Tilly sat upright and saw trees pressing in unnaturally closely, their branches and leaves scratching and scraping at the windows as the train rushed by. She looked around, searching for signs of worry among the other passengers, but everyone else was absorbed in their phones or books, or snoozing. Her breathing started to quicken in panic as the darkness closed in, casting the whole train into shadow, and yet still no one else seemed to react. A cracking noise like boots on a frozen lake echoed in Tilly's ears, and she shrank back as a tree branch that suddenly seemed conscious and full of intent snaked its way through the window, as if the glass just wasn't there, and curled its way up and across the ceiling of the train. More and more branches followed it, filling the train with treacherous ropes of bark. Tilly watched in terror as a sinuous branch crept under her feet and across the aisle toward an elderly man sleeping with his mouth slightly ajar.

"Stop!" Tilly shouted, panicked. "Wake up!" She flung herself across the seats and onto the sleeping man, trying to grab at the branch before it suffocated him.

"What on earth do you think you're doing?" the man spluttered.

"I was stopping the trees!" she said, but the moment the words were out of her mouth, the trees were nowhere to be seen. They had simply vanished, and wintery sun was spilling through the windows. The man was looking at her with concern.

"What trees?" he said.

"I'm so sorry," Tilly said, face burning with embarrassment, as she retreated across the aisle to her seat. Tilly pressed her face against the window, trying to catch a glimpse of the forest, but it was nowhere to be seen.

Pages and Co.
The
Lost Fairy Tales

Anna James

Illustrated by
Paola Escobar

PUFFIN BOOKS

PUFFIN BOOKS
An imprint of Penguin Random House LLC, New York

First published in the United States of America by Philomel Books,
an imprint of Penguin Random House LLC, 2020
First published as *Tilly and the Lost Fairy Tales* in Great Britain by HarperCollins Children's Books, in 2019
Published by Puffin Books, an imprint of Penguin Random House LLC, 2021

Text copyright © 2019 by Anna James
Illustrations copyright © 2019 by Paola Escobar
Teaser of *Pages & Co.: The Map of Stories* copyright © 2020 by Anna James

Visit us online at penguinrandomhouse.com.

THE LIBRARY OF CONGRESS HAS CATALOGED THE PHILOMEL BOOKS EDITION AS FOLLOWS:
Names: James, Anna (Anna Lois), author. | Escobar, Paola, illustrator.
Title: The lost fairy tales / Anna James ; illustrated by Paola Escobar.
Other titles: Tilly and the lost fairy tales
Description: U.S. edition. | New York : Philomel Books, 2020.
Series: Pages & Co. ; 2 | "First published as Tilly and the Lost Fairy Tales in Great Britain
by HarperCollins Children's Books in 2019." | Audience: Ages 8–12. | Audience: Grades 4–6. |
Summary: When eleven-year-old Tilly Pages joins Oskar
and his family on a Christmas trip to Paris, she and her friend bookwander into the land of
fairy tales, where someone—or something—is causing chaos.
Identifiers: LCCN 2019056886 | ISBN 9781984837295 (hardcover) | ISBN 9781984837301 (ebk)
Subjects: CYAC: Books and reading—Fiction. | Characters in literature—Fiction.
Bookstores—Fiction. | Magic—Fiction. | Grandparents—Fiction. | Missing persons—Fiction.
Paris (France)—Fiction. | France—Fiction.
Classification: LCC PZ7.1.J3847 Los 2020 | DDC [Fic]—dc23
LC record available at https://lccn.loc.gov/2019056886

Printed in the USA

Puffin Books ISBN 9781984837318

3 5 7 9 10 8 6 4 2

US edition edited by Cheryl Eissing • US edition designed by Ellice M. Lee
Text set in Adobe Caslon

For my mum and dad,
who have always let me find my own path

1

A Little Magic

Five people proved to be far too many to fit inside a wardrobe.

"Remind me again why we had to bookwander from in here?" Tilly asked, face squished uncomfortably close to her grandad's shoulder.

"As I rather think you know," he replied, "we don't *technically* have to bookwander from inside a wardrobe—but it adds effect, don't you think?" But he sounded decidedly less sure than when he'd first suggested the idea half an hour ago.

"I mean, if the effect you're going for is a much closer relationship with each other and our personal hygiene choices, then yes, it does add effect," Oskar said, voice muffled by Grandma's scarf, which was simultaneously tickling his nose and getting fluff in his mouth every time he spoke.

"I bet the Pevensies didn't have to deal with this," Tilly said.

"Yes, but they were emptying straight out the other side of their wardrobe," Grandma said. "Which does rather give them an advantage."

"Yes, yes, okay," Grandad admitted. "It has become abundantly clear that my attempts at a little poetry and whimsy weren't entirely thought through." He shuffled his way back toward the door and shoved it open. Tilly; her best friend, Oskar; her two grandparents; and her mother all fell gasping into the cinnamon-scented air of the bookshop.

"I mean, it isn't even a wardrobe," Oskar complained. "It's a stock cupboard."

"Honestly," Grandad huffed. "I was just trying to add a sense of adventure. Mirror the journey into Narnia, have some fun. Goodness knows we could all do with a generous dollop of fun at the moment. A little magic."

"It's already literally magic," Tilly pointed out.

"I'm wasted on this family, I truly am," Grandad said. "Shall we try again from out here? We've still got an hour or so before we need to go to the Underlibrary for the Inking Ceremony."

"Actually, Dad, I think I might pass on this one," Tilly's mum, Bea, said quietly, smoothing down her crumpled clothes. "The shop is so busy before Christmas, and I'm sure an extra pair of hands wouldn't go amiss. You know how it is. . . ." She trailed off, smiled wanly, and headed out to Pages & Co., the bookshop the Pages family lived in and owned. Tilly sagged a little.

"She hasn't bookwandered once since we got back from

A Little Princess," Tilly said, trying not to sound petulant.

"I know, sweetheart, but try not to worry," Grandad said. "I'm sure she'll get back into it soon enough. It's no surprise after being trapped inside one story for nearly twelve years. Imagine how frightening that must have been for her." As always, when he thought about his daughter being imprisoned inside a tampered-with copy of *A Little Princess*, a look of distress swept across his face. "But we've got her back for good," he went on. "And now that we know Enoch Chalk was the one who trapped her, he won't be able to get away with anything like that ever again."

"If he's ever found," Tilly pointed out.

"Did Amelia manage to find out anything about the book he escaped from before she was fired?" Oskar asked.

"Amelia wasn't fired," Grandad said. "She was asked to step back from her position as Head Librarian at the Underlibrary while the situation is investigated properly."

"I mean, that sounds a lot like getting fired to me," Oskar said under his breath.

"And, in answer to your question: no, frustratingly not," Grandma said. "She barely had any time before the Bookbinders started poisoning the other librarians' views about her capabilities. They'd been looking for a reason to get rid of her as soon as she was first given the job, and her handling of Chalk was merely an excuse. Those hard-liners, with their silly, self-important—not to mention self-appointed—name, blustering around pretending they were focused on anything other than their own power and influence." Grandad laid a hand on Grandma's arm and she took a deep breath. "Sorry," she said. "Now is not the time, and here is not the place."

"Should I know who the Bookbinders are?" Oskar said, and Tilly was glad, not for the first time, that he didn't mind asking about what he didn't know.

"They are nonsense!" Grandad said. "A group of librarians who push for stricter rules and for more control for the Underlibrary over the lives of bookwanderers. They rallied around Chalk—although they must be red-faced now that everyone knows he was a renegade Source character. But embarrassment often pushes people several more steps down the path toward hatred, and I worry that their championing of a colleague who proved to be fictional is fuel for their witch hunt of Amelia."

"Nonsense they may be," Grandma said. "But they're bringing an alarming number of librarians over to their ways of thinking. People are worried about how the role of the Underlibrary is evolving, and fear is another thing that pulls people toward hatred."

"Aren't the librarians worried about where Chalk is?" Oskar said. "Isn't it dangerous for him to be out there somewhere?"

"I think they're torn between concern about what he is

up to and wanting to sweep it under the carpet so the other Underlibraries don't find out."

"The other Underlibraries?" Oskar asked. "In other countries, you mean?"

"Yes," Grandad said. "There are Underlibraries in most countries, although not all of them have Source Libraries. But I think that's enough politics for now; we have a long afternoon ahead of us, which will likely be even more draining than an eternal winter ruled over by an evil queen. Let's have something to eat."

A lunch of scrambled eggs and sliced avocado on hot buttered bagels passed in tentative silence. Although they initially tried to maintain conversation, Grandma and Grandad were firmly inside their own heads, and a vague sense of impending doom hung over the table. The squeak of knives on plates and the sound of the dishwasher whirring in the background were all that could be heard for some time.

"Is it really that bad?" Oskar asked nervously, trying to break the silence. "I feel like we're about to go to a funeral."

"Well, it's certainly a funeral for our dear Amelia's career," Grandad grumped. "Not to mention potentially the death of British bookwandering as we know it."

"That does sound *quite* bad, then," Oskar said.

"Come now, Archie," Grandma said. "Leaving aside our personal sadness for Amelia, this is not quite so dramatic as all of that. Bookwandering will continue; the British Underlibrary will continue. These things come in waves. You know that there was always going to be pushback against Amelia's approach—those old-fashioned cronies were always angry that someone with more forward-facing ideas got the Librarian job when several of them had been hankering after it. Life will go on as usual; it always does."

"Until, of course, it doesn't," Grandad said ominously. Grandma gave him a stern "not in front of the children" look and he harrumphed, pushing his chair back with a squeal. He sullenly dumped his dirty plate by the sink, and turned to leave—before heading back sheepishly and washing it up carefully without making eye contact with anyone.

Once the rest of the lunch things had been cleared away and everyone had checked for crumbs on their nice clothes, they traipsed out of Pages & Co., leaving Bea in charge for the afternoon.

"Are you sure you two want to come?" Grandad checked.

"Yes," Oskar and Tilly chorused, not sure there'd ever be a bookwandering scenario that they would choose to miss out on.

"I haven't explicitly checked with the Underlibrary that you're allowed," he said, as if that thought had just occurred to him. "But they're hardly going to turn you away if you're already there, are they?" he concluded, more to himself than anyone else.

"I know it's sad for Amelia," Tilly said. "But I do want to see what happens when a new Librarian is chosen."

"You said there was a vote?" Oskar asked.

"Yes," Grandma said. "Anyone who wants to put themselves forward for the position can make their case, and then it's up to the other librarians to choose who they think is most suited for the role."

"So you were voted for?" Tilly asked her grandad.

"He won over thirteen other candidates!" Grandma said proudly.

"How many are there this time?" Oskar asked.

"Only three, I believe," Grandma said. "It would seem the situation with Chalk has rather cooled some people's ambitions. Who would want to be in charge of that mess? So I believe there's Ebenezer Okparanta—who's worked at the Underlibrary since time began as far as I know—and a woman, Catherine Caraway, who's a bit of a wild card. . . ."

"And then there's Melville Underwood," Grandad said. "He's an interesting character. Disappeared for decades with his sister, Decima, not long after I started working at the Underlibrary, and no one thought we'd ever see them again. They used to run fairy-tale tours for bookwanderers, and all sorts can go on in those stories. But he emerged again a couple of weeks ago, completely out of the blue, and without his sister. I'm sure he'll talk about his triumphant return in his speech, but he's a bit untested for the job. I'd put money on them electing Ebenezer. He's the safe bet, and I'm not sure this is the time for surprises."

2

Fairy Tales Are Funny Things

Grandad had booked a taxi to King's Cross, and the sleek black car waiting on the street outside the bookshop did not help with the funereal atmosphere.

"You said one of the candidates used to run fairy-tale tours?" Tilly asked, wondering about the unusual phrase her grandad had used. "What does that even mean?"

"Well, fairy tales are funny things," Grandad said. "Do you know where they come from? Who wrote them?"

"The Brothers . . . something?" Oskar tried.

"The Brothers Grimm," Tilly said authoritatively. "And Hans Christian Andersen. Lots of people."

"You're right—but that's not the whole story," Grandad said. "Those people did indeed write many fairy tales down, and put their own spin on them for sure, but they didn't make up most of the stories themselves—they collected them. Fairy tales and folktales are born around campfires and kitchen hearths;

they're whispered under blankets and stars. Where they really come from, who had the idea first, which version is the original, it's almost impossible to trace, as we only have what was written down, which is rarely where they started."

"And can you think about why that might make them more dangerous?" Grandma asked.

"Because . . ." Tilly started confidently, but to her frustration couldn't think of anything. Oskar sat deep in thought.

"Is it something to do with Source Editions?" he said. "Usually when something is dangerous in bookwandering, it's to do with that."

"Yes, you're getting warmer," Grandma said. "Keep going."

"If there's lots of different versions . . ." Tilly said.

". . . and we don't know where they came from . . ." Oskar continued.

". . . then are there even Source Editions at all?" Tilly finished.

"Precisely," Grandad said. "We have Source Editions of many of the different versions, of course, that act loosely like Sources, but these stories aren't rooted in written-down storytelling. They come from oral storytelling, stories that are told out loud and passed down generations and around communities."

"And roots are what make things stable," Grandma went on. "Fairy tales are rooted in air and fire, not paper and ink, so the usual rules don't apply. Layers of stories bleed or crash into each other and you can end up wandering into an entirely different version of the story with little way of getting out. It's incredibly dangerous to try to wander from inside one story to another; it's like trying to find a route on a map but you don't know where you're starting from. Not to mention, fables fade in and out of existence; we tell new versions and we lose old ones. So they're seen as a bit of a risk for bookwandering. Sometimes the Underlibrary would organize group visits led by someone who was a bit more comfortable there and understood the risks and what to do to stay safe—or try to stay safe."

"Have you been inside any fairy tales? Can you take us?" Tilly asked. Her grandparents exchanged a look and she couldn't help but wish they weren't quite so good at communicating without speaking. She wondered if she would ever be a team like that with someone, and experimented by glaring at Oskar meaningfully.

"Are . . . are you okay?" he asked nervously. "You look like you need to sneeze."

"Never mind," she said, blushing and turning back to Grandma and Grandad. "You didn't answer my question."

"Actually, your grandma is one of the few bookwanderers who does bookwander in fairy tales officially and safely," Grandad said, looking at her proudly.

"How come?" Oskar said.

"Well, as you both know, I used to work in the Map Room at the Underlibrary," Grandma said. "And as well as looking after the plans of real-life bookshops and libraries, it was also part of my job to know as much as I could about the layout of stories themselves. I did a bit of fairy-tale exploring back in the day, but that project was abandoned after . . . well, after a difference of opinion, let's say."

Tilly thought about her grandma, who always took everything in stride, and was intrigued. "There's got to be more to that story," she pushed.

"But it will have to be told another time," Grandad said. "We're here."

3

Slightly on the Outside

To Tilly's eyes, the steady stream of people in matching navy-blue cardigans weren't doing a very good job of being inconspicuous inside the British Library. But despite the coordinated clothing and loud whispering, they didn't seem to be attracting much attention from the regular library users.

"They'll assume it's a tour group," Grandad said as they walked through the "Staff Only" door that led inside the King's Library, a glass-wrapped tower of books in the middle of the main hall. "People are good at not noticing things that don't affect them. How do you think we've hidden a magical library here for decades?"

There was a line to access the seemingly out-of-order lift that carried bookwanderers down from the main library and into the British Underlibrary. Tilly had expected the mood to be somber, as it had been at Pages & Co., but there was a disconcerting buzz in the air, and lots of excited faces in the crowd.

"Aren't we supposed to be sad?" Oskar whispered to Tilly.

"We are," Tilly said, "because Amelia is our friend, but I guess lots of people are cross with her for keeping what she knew about Chalk a secret."

"We are . . . on the right side, yes?" Oskar said.

"Side of what?" Tilly asked.

"Whatever this is," Oskar said. "Because it is clearly something." And although Tilly was loath to admit it to herself, she had to accept that Oskar was right. A now-familiar panic rose in Tilly's chest. The feeling of belonging and acceptance she'd experienced when she first found out she was a bookwanderer had been ripped away when she discovered that she was half-fictional. She was of their world and yet removed from it, and sometimes felt like one of those children she'd read about in novels who were forced to live inside a plastic bubble because they were sick and couldn't risk contamination—as though she had to keep parts of herself hidden and protected. And now there were all these complicated Underlibrary politics she couldn't quite grasp, and there was a tiny voice in the back of her head asking whether everything would be easier if she'd never found out she was a bookwanderer at all. Who wanted to be special anyway? All it seemed to mean was secrets, suspicious looks, and a feeling of always being slightly on the outside.

Despite this, and the strange atmosphere crackling in

the Underlibrary, Tilly couldn't help but feel a sudden rush of wonder at the sight of the beautiful main hall that stretched high above her head, with its turquoise ceiling and sweeping wooden arches. A librarian rushed over to them and shook Grandad's hand vigorously.

"Seb!" Oskar said happily, recognizing the librarian who had helped them learn how to bookwander a few months ago.

"How are you all? Mr. Pages, sir, Ms. Pages, lovely to see you," Seb said. "Tilly, Oskar." He was speaking incredibly quickly, unable to stop himself being polite, despite clearly having something very important to say. "If you wouldn't mind following me, Amelia's waiting for you." He shepherded the four of them off into an anteroom, keeping an eye on who was watching them go. The room he took them to was lined with bookshelves and warmed by a large fire, and pacing in front of it was Amelia Whisper, the former Head Librarian, her long black hair pinned up into a formal hairstyle that robbed her of some of her usual warmth. Her skin, usually a glowing brown, looked paler and duller than normal. She nodded to them as they came in.

"Thank you for coming," she said.

"Of course, Amelia," Grandma said, rushing across the room and trying to wrap her in a hug, which Amelia stopped with a firm hand.

"Don't be too kind to me," Amelia said. "You'll make me cry, which is not very on brand for me at all. And I need to talk to you about something much more important than me and my feelings. Seb and I are worried about what's going on here."

"Well, we all are," Grandad said. "Honestly, insisting you stand down, listening to these cliques and their harebrained ideas."

"No, I mean something more than that," Amelia said. "Yes, I'm heartbroken that the Underlibrary is choosing to replace me, but, well, they're within their rights to do so."

"Barely," Grandad muttered.

"But the issue is whom they're replacing me with. Or trying to."

"What do you mean?" Grandma asked.

"I don't trust Melville Underwood at all, and I think there's more to his story than he's letting on."

"Ah, but they won't go for him, surely," Grandad said. "He's just gotten back from goodness knows where. No one knows anything about him. It'll be old Ebenezer."

"I'm not so sure," Amelia said. "You haven't been here over the last week; Melville may have just gotten back, but he's been darting around the Library whispering in people's ears, and I'm worried about what he's saying, and what people are open to believing. I don't think it's a coincidence that the Bookbinders have stopped grumbling from the sidelines and started to get more organized."

"If I could be permitted to chip in," Seb said. "I am a little concerned about where he has been all this time, as you say, Mr. Pages—but others don't share our reservations. The Bookbinders, as they insist on calling themselves now, are lapping up Melville's tale because they are happy to gloss over all sorts of irregularities if it means having one of their own in charge. Ideologically, I mean. Better the devil you sort of know, and all that. But while he claims that he and his sister were attacked while leading a book-wandering group through a collection of fairy tales, there are no records of this attack happening. If a group of bookwanderers was attacked or lost, there should be some note or diary or even a personal memory somewhere in our records. He says he can't be sure what happened to the rest of the group, or his sister, and no one seems to be pushing him on it. Something smells fishy to me."

"But there's no proof?" Grandad said slowly.

"Well, no," Seb said. "The lack of evidence or proof is just the issue. There's no way to corroborate his story. We're a group of librarians and archivists and storytellers; why aren't we more concerned that there's no record . . . ?"

"I do worry that unfounded claims such as these will merely make us look like sore losers, especially today," Grandad said slowly. "Is there wisdom in waiting and watching for a while, do you think? I must admit, I never warmed to Melville when I crossed paths with him back when we were both young men here."

"That's the other thing," Amelia said. "He's still a young man."

"Well, that's nothing of note in itself," Grandma said. "Aging works erratically in books as it is, and if he was in fairy tales, then even more so."

"Yes, but he doesn't seem to have aged a day," Amelia said. "He still looks to be in his late twenties."

"My dear Amelia, it's easy to find evidence of what we already believe. . . ."

Amelia brushed Grandad's reassuring hand off her arm.

"Don't you dare patronize me, Archie," she said. "I am not some conspiracy theorist; I know the Underlibrary of today better than you do. I understand that we are dealing with little more than smoke and whispers and instincts here."

"You know what they say about no smoke without fire," Seb said sagely.

Amelia ignored him. "There is something else happening here," she said firmly, "and you would be wise to take my warning seriously."

Grandad nodded, chastened. "You're right," he said. "I'm sorry, I didn't mean to . . . I just, well, Elsie and I both care for you greatly as our friend and colleague, and I don't want to see you get hurt more than necessary."

"The hurt is already inflicted," Amelia said, steely-eyed. "And I can endure it. But I want it to be worth something, and it is time for some answers. Do you know, in recent weeks I have found myself wondering if I was ever really quite cut out for being in charge? Do you think I'd make a good rebel? I'm interested to see if I've got it in me." There was a definite twinkle in her eye. "Now, if only I can convince Seb to start disobeying some rules . . ."

"One step at a time," Seb said, breaking out in a light sweat at the mere thought.

4

A Less Than Ideal Situation

Seb led them back to the main hall. A table and a microphone had been set up on a sturdy platform at one end of the hall, and rows of chairs faced it. On top of the table was an enormous book bound in ruby-red leather beside an old-fashioned inkpot complete with a feathered quill. Librarians had nearly filled up the rows, but Seb ushered Grandad, Grandma, Tilly, and Oskar to reserved seats near the front. As they sat down, Tilly couldn't help but notice the way everyone turned to look at them, undisguised suspicion on many faces. Was it her or her grandparents who were attracting such distrust? Or all of them?

"Considering our part in the whole Enoch Chalk debacle, I'm surprised we're up here at the front," Grandad whispered.

"All the better to keep an eye on us, I'm sure," Grandma said.

"You know how it is," Seb said. "Tradition always wins out,

and tradition states that any living former Librarians are guests of honor at Inking Ceremonies. And I imagine that if you don't bring Chalk up, no one else will. People are happy to let Amelia take the fall for this; it's easier to blame one person than to think about what's really happening."

Tilly was distracted from people's suspicious glares when she noticed a young man emerge and stand just behind the platform, eyes closed, talking to himself under his breath. He had neat white-blond hair and was wearing a navy-blue suit, with a librarian cardigan underneath the jacket. He looked very focused, and Tilly could only assume it was Melville Underwood, the man who Amelia and Seb were so wary of. Behind him, talking to each other amiably, were a very old man with a silvery beard that curled its way down to his shins and a middle-aged woman in a wheelchair wearing all black. As Tilly watched, a librarian came up behind Melville and startled him out of his meditations with a tap to the shoulder. She spoke quietly to him, gesturing at the microphone, and Tilly saw a flash of irritation cross his face, quickly replaced by a warm, polished smile. She nudged Grandad.

"That's him, isn't it?" she asked.

Grandad looked up and nodded. "And the man with the beard is Ebenezer, and the woman is Catherine," he said as the three candidates and Amelia came and sat facing the audience. Amelia kept her head held high, her brow furrowed.

The crowd hushed as one, as if responding to an invisible

signal, and only the occasional creak of a wooden chair echoed through the hall. A man who looked like he worked in a bank rather than a magical library climbed the steps onto the platform and tapped the microphone hesitantly, causing a shriek of feedback to bounce around the room. The audience grimaced, and the man blushed.

"That's Cassius McCray," Grandad whispered to Tilly and Oskar. "Chief Secretary of the Underlibrary."

Cassius didn't apologize, just glared at the microphone as though it were personally trying to undermine him. He cleared his throat.

"Right," he started. "Well, we are gathered here today for the Inking Ceremony. This is a slightly unusual situation due to the, uh, circumstances. As you all know, our former colleague Enoch Chalk was revealed to be a, well, a fictional character from a Source Edition. He had been working here undetected for decades, trapping anyone who discovered him in books that he had tampered with. It was a . . . a less than ideal situation. Ms. Whisper, our former Head Librarian, had her suspicions about his true nature and decided not to share them with us, her colleagues.

We believe that decision makes her, well, unsuitable for that esteemed role, and she has been relieved of her duties. We thank Ms. Whisper for her service to the British Underlibrary, and we have offered her another, more suitable, position here should she wish to remain and make amends by helping us discover the whereabouts of Mr. Chalk. That investigation is ongoing, and we are confident it will be resolved satisfactorily. We will, of course, keep you updated. As is our duty."

Throughout this, Amelia kept her chin in the air with no trace of penitence on her face. Tilly felt as though she wanted to applaud her, or run up and hug her, or do anything at all to show her she was on Amelia's side. And there it was again in her head: the idea of sides, and of having to be on one.

"Well," Cassius continued, "this of course means we must elect a new Librarian, and we have had three, uh, yes, three candidates put themselves forward, and despite their, shall we say, current status, it is in our statutes that anyone who is eligible may speak to us. So, we will hear from all three and there will be the opportunity to put questions to them and then, as is tradition, we will have a private ballot to determine Ms. Whisper's successor. So, uh, shall we start with our dear friend Ebenezer Okparanta . . . ?" A librarian behind him coughed and Cassius corrected himself. "I mean, our colleague Ebenezer Okparanta."

The old man with the long silvery beard took to the stage, a warm smile on his face.

"My friends," he began. "For we are all dear friends here.

I stand before you an old man, but one who wishes to unite us all under the principles we hold so dear. We are in a time of confusion and tumult, but it needn't continue. We care for a magical and important thing here, and we are being distracted from our purpose by infighting and egos. We must continue our work to prevent the closure of bookshops and libraries while also working to protect ourselves and our community—two goals that can be achieved in harmony. I believe, at this juncture, my long past here at the Underlibrary and proven dedication to our goals make me the steady hand we need to steer us through this time. I have worked with you all for many years, and I hope that my experience speaks for itself. Thank you, friends."

"Any questions?" Cassius said, and hands sprang up.

"Ebenezer, what are you going to do about Enoch Chalk?" a voice said.

"I shall, of course, be working with Amelia to find out where he has gone, and—"

"But," interrupted the voice, "I think, or rather I *know*, there are others here who believe that librarians should be tested to ensure we are all who we say we are."

"Why, no," Ebenezer said, sounding surprised. "I haven't heard that. What do we have without trust in each other?"

"Look where that's gotten us," another voice said in a stage whisper, and Ebenezer started to look slightly flummoxed.

"Enoch needs to be dealt with, of course, my friends, but there are bigger things at play," he said. "The waning of book magic as bookshops and libraries close, the erratic readings we're getting from fairy tales."

"Let's hear from Melville Underwood!" a woman cried. "He's been inside the fairy tales, after all!"

"Now, now," Cassius said. "It's Catherine's turn next. Let's just leave it there with Ebenezer."

Ebenezer walked offstage a little wobbily, clearly taken aback by the mood in the room, and was replaced by the woman wheeling herself up the ramp onto the stage.

"That's Catherine Caraway," Grandma whispered.

"Fellow bookwanderers," Catherine said, sounding confident and warm. "For too long we have neglected our primary reason for existence and have been mired in bureaucracy. I want to lead an Underlibrary that is focused on bookwandering. What we need to do is contact the Archivists." Tilly could hear tutting spread through the room, and even a few derisive laughs. "We have abandoned them for too long," Catherine went on, her voice building in volume. "Why are we so surprised they have forsaken us? Let us give our problems to them to resolve, and get back to our true purpose."

Tilly glanced at her grandparents and saw that they both looked deeply uncomfortable, as though Catherine had suggested enlisting the Easter Bunny to help.

"Who would you choose?" Tilly whispered to Grandma.

"Leaving aside the obvious fact that Amelia is considerably more suitable than any of them," she said quietly, "Ebenezer's heart is in the right place, I am sure, but I worry he doesn't have the strength to cope with rebel voices here. And goodness knows what Catherine is talking about. She's showing her naivety. . . ."

"But couldn't the Archivists help?" Tilly said. "I thought they were, like, the most important bookwanderers?"

"Trusting in the Archivists is like relying on a unicorn to come and grant you wishes to solve your problems," Grandma replied.

"Maybe Melville will be better?" Tilly whispered, stealing another glance at the man who was watching Catherine field increasingly angry questions with a look of sincere, polite interest on his face.

"We shall see," Grandma said, and then they were shushed by someone sitting behind them.

Catherine wheeled her chair down from the stage and Cassius took the microphone again, looking very unsettled. Amelia tried—and failed—to keep a slightly smug expression off her face.

"Right, well," Cassius spluttered. "Let's just remember we're all colleagues, shall we? So, where were we . . . ? Yes, well, finally, we have our rather last-minute candidate. A long-lost wanderer has unexpectedly returned to us and has put himself forward, which he is absolutely permitted to do. Some of you who have been here awhile will remember our colleagues the Underwood twins. Melville and Decima were bookwanderers in the field, putting their own lives on the line to explore the limits of our stories in fairy tales. When they vanished without a trace, we believed they had made, well, the ultimate sacrifice for their work in some of our most dangerous stories. But . . . a miracle has occurred, and we are encouraged by the return of Mr. Melville Underwood."

Cassius climbed down from the platform, and Melville Underwood took to the stage. The silence in the room was absolute and Tilly found herself leaning forward, eager to hear what he would say.

"My friends," Melville started. His voice sounded as though it had been dipped in honey. "I am so grateful to have found my way back to you. I have endured years balancing on the brink of survival in the fairy-tale worlds, alone in my grief for my poor sister, Decima. The thought of coming home, to my British Underlibrary family, has sustained me. Although I have come close to the most dangerous elements of bookwandering, my experiences have not diminished my love for it. Indeed, they have, if anything, deepened my respect and awe for the book-wandering magic we are so fortunate to use. But that magic is by no means guaranteed, and I have witnessed firsthand, and learned from my esteemed friends here, that there are signs that this precious magic is becoming unpredictable. At this time, we need to band together and protect bookwandering while we still can." He looked around the room, assessing how his words were going down, his eyes lingering just a second too long as he noticed Grandma and Grandad.

"British bookwandering has long been at the heart of the whole global community, and we must keep it this way," he continued. "Now that the fairy-tale lands are increasingly unstable, I fear whatever is causing that will spread to our other stories. We must be vigilant! I, as we all should be, am grateful to Amelia for her work leading our community for the last decade, but the time has come for a different approach. We simply cannot allow incidents like the Enoch Chalk disaster to happen. It has threatened the very principles by which we live. I would ask us to unite! Unite in the face of instability and threats to the power and sanctity of our stories—and the British Underlibrary itself. I agree with both of my esteemed colleagues: Ebenezer is right that we must come together, and Catherine raises important points about our core purpose. I am grounded in both of these principles, but I hope that my time in the fairy-tale lands—on the front line of our storytelling—has given me the clarity and purpose needed at this moment in our history. We have such wisdom and experience among our fellow British Underlibrarians. As well as Ebenezer and Catherine, I understand that while I have been away, some of our colleagues have been diligent in their research into the best ways to preserve and protect bookwandering under the ancestral name of the Bookbinders. If I were so fortunate as to be elected, I would be honored to work alongside them, and you all, to unite us in the most effective and efficient ways of ensuring characters—and bookwanderers—are less likely to go astray!" He smiled to the crowd, like they were all in on the same joke. "Now, I'll be happy to answer any questions you may have," he finished. "And I appreciate you will have many." A round of polite, appreciative applause rippled across the hall, and Tilly saw a flicker of anxiety run across Amelia's face.

"Thank you, friends," Melville said graciously.

Grandad raised his hand.

"Tell me, Melville. Why are you the right person to lead now?" he said. "When you have not been with us for so many years? Could you not stay and learn and observe, and look to take the helm in the future?" Grandad's voice was ice-cold, despite the politeness of his words.

"Well, Archibald," Melville said, smiling at Grandad, "I believe that I can offer much to the Underlibrary, as I have just set out. But there is one other thing, something that I had not planned to mention, as it should not have any bearing on the election here today. But as you have forced my hand, Archibald, and in answer to your excellent question, let me share something with you now. I come to you not just armed with information about how we can save our beloved fairy tales, but also with incontrovertible evidence as to

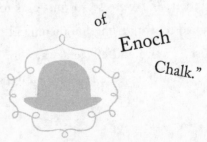

the whereabouts

of

Enoch

Chalk."

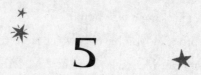

5

Something Strange Is Afoot

There was a second of absolute silence, before the room erupted into chaos. People were gesturing wildly and shouting over each other. Melville simply surveyed the crowd with a look of complete calm on his face. Tilly felt cold all over and saw Grandma and Grandad exchange ominous looks.

"Now, see here," Cassius spluttered into the microphone. "That's quite a thing to claim, Melville. What do you know? You are obliged to share it with us, you must see that!"

"Of course," Melville said, quieting the crowd with one hand raised. "I did not want to sway the feelings of my colleagues at this delicate point; that is the only reason I did not mention it before. But I am eager to share what I have learned with you all. While on my travels searching for a way back from the fairy-tale lands, I happened across several characters complaining of a man being discourteous and poking around, asking questions. I attempted to find him myself, assuming he was a bookwanderer seeking a way home."

"What proof do you have?" a voice from the back called.

"Will you permit me a moment?" Melville asked Cassius, who nodded helplessly as Melville slipped offstage and returned a few moments later with a cardboard box in his hand. The tension in the air was electric as he set the box down on the desk.

"Will this suffice as proof?" And with one hand he pulled out a gray bowler hat that was unmistakably Enoch Chalk's.

A brief pause hung in the air, and then the majority of the audience started applauding loudly. Amelia raised an eyebrow at Grandad.

"Isn't that a good thing?" Tilly whispered to Grandma, confused. "I thought we wanted to find Chalk. Doesn't that prove Mr. Underwood is on our side?"

"Perhaps," Grandma said. "But perhaps not. I don't trust Melville, but I do trust Amelia's instincts. There are many questions unanswered—how would Melville know Chalk was a threat in the first place? And we—of course—want Chalk found and dealt with, and we may align with Melville on other things, too. Who knows. The one thing I *am* sure of is that something strange is afoot."

Cassius was back onstage, trying to calm everyone down again.

"I think . . . I think the only thing we can do now is vote," he said. "We will invite you up a row at a time to cast your ballot, so please return to your chairs until you're called, and, well, we shall go from there. Current employees of the Underlibrary only," he added, looking directly at Grandad, who rolled his eyes. There was a lot of hushed conversation as, row by row, nearly fifty librarians filed up to the front, marked a piece of paper, and posted it through a large wooden casket, all under Cassius's flustered glare. Once everyone had voted, Cassius and another librarian carried the ballot box out of the hall. Half an hour later, Cassius returned, looking slightly pale.

"We have counted and verified—more than once—the votes, and I am, well, I am happy, yes, to announce that the next Librarian of the British Underlibrary will be Melville Underwood."

There was thunderous applause as the name was announced, although, as Tilly craned her neck, she could see small pockets of librarians who weren't clapping at all. But the mood was undeniably in Melville's favor, and he approached the stage once more, still clutching Chalk's hat in his hand.

"I look forward to working for you," he said, bowing his head humbly as the applause washed over him. Once it had died down a little, Cassius approached, and Melville took off his suit jacket and rolled up his cardigan and shirtsleeves. A librarian had opened the book, and smoothed the pages down reverently.

"So he just signs his name now and he's the Head Librarian?" Tilly asked.

"There's a little more commitment than that required," Grandad said. "You guys aren't squeamish, right?"

"Nope," Oskar said, craning to make sure he had a good view. Cassius stepped forward and looked at Melville, who gave a firm nod and held out his hand for the quill.

"The ink of the Underlibrary represents our stories, which are now part of you," Cassius said formally. He took Melville's wrist and held his fingers over the inkpot before quickly and firmly pricking his finger with the quill, and letting a drop of blood fall into the ink below. Tilly was watching Melville's face, and he swallowed but didn't make a sound. "And by giving a drop of your blood, you are now part of the Underlibrary," Cassius continued, handing Melville the quill, which he dipped into the ink before signing the great book on the table. "With this Inking Ceremony, the lifeblood of both you and the Underlibrary are one and the same." Cassius shook Melville's other hand, and Melville's face broke into a wide, warm smile. He pulled Cassius into a one-sided embrace, breaking the solemn mood of the moment.

"Was that it?" Oskar said, sounding a little disappointed.

"Did Amelia have to do that?" Tilly asked Grandma.

"Why, yes," she said. "And your grandad, too, of course." Grandad smiled and held up the ring finger on his right hand, where a tiny, faded **black** dot was visible.

"Isn't that dangerous?" Tilly asked. "Won't you get, like, ink-poisoned or something by it?"

"Oh no," Grandma said. "It's just like getting a tiny tattoo, really."

"And I seem to be doing all right so far," Grandad said, smiling and absentmindedly rubbing the pad of his finger where the tiny mark was. "Now, let's get out of here before we have to make any awkward small talk. I could use a cup of tea."

"Not so fast," a voice cut in. They turned to see Cassius standing by their seats. "Melville would like to have a word. With all of you."

6

Riddles and Obfuscation

The group followed Cassius back into the room where they had been talking before the ceremony. The fire had been stoked into a roaring blaze and the room was stiflingly hot. Seb, who was sticking to them like toffee, followed silently and closed the door behind them. The only person who still looked fresh and comfortable was Melville Underwood, who was sitting in a leather armchair right in front of the fire, a neat bandage wrapped around the tip of his finger. The charming man who had spoken at the Inking Ceremony had evaporated and his face was stern as he observed them.

"Good to see you again, Melville," Grandad said in the voice he used when he meant precisely the opposite of the words coming out his mouth. "How on earth do you have Chalk's hat? You claim a moment of heroism, yet surely when you met him, you had no idea who he was? There's no need for secrets at this stage. We're all on the same side, right?"

"I have a few orders of business to get through," Melville said, ignoring Grandad. "Firstly, while you have been invited here as a courtesy to your previous role, Archibald, you and your family are no longer welcome at the British Underlibrary except in cases of extreme bookwandering emergencies or at my personal invitation."

"You can't do that!" Oskar said, outraged. "Can you?"

"Who are you?" Melville said as if he had just noticed Oskar.

"I'm Oskar, obviously, and you should know who I am because I helped rescue Tilly's mum last year and find out the truth about Chalk."

"Ah, you were the other child who allowed him to escape through your meddling," Melville said coldly. "Of course there is no need to worry about that anymore. We will be bringing him to justice shortly."

"So where is he?" Tilly asked.

"That is none of your concern," Melville said dismissively. "Why two children have already become so involved in this issue is beyond me. Your inability to see the big picture, let alone put it before your own personal vendettas and childish desire for adventure, is what's gotten us here, with this dangerous man on the loose."

"Good grief, Underwood," Grandad said. "You know it's not their fault—beneath all your posturing, you can't get away from the fact that without Tilly and Oskar, none of us would have realized that Chalk was an escaped Source character. Now, will you tell us why you have the man's hat? This is no time for riddles and obfuscation."

"That's the second time in mere hours that I've had to repeat myself to you. You must try to be a better listener, Archibald," Melville responded icily. "As I said, I was aided by characters in the fairy-tale land. As I searched for a way out, I had heard rumors about a man asking questions, and I assumed he was an errant bookwanderer. I had hoped I would be able to wander back to the real world with him. But when I found him, he was instantly combative and refused to talk to me, just muttered on and on about some nonsense I couldn't understand. Once I'd realized he wasn't in his right mind, I distracted him and slipped a book out from his pocket to ensure my escape route. Naturally, I attempted to bring him with me, but he resisted and ran away, leaving only his hat on the ground. I picked it up in the hopes of identifying him when I'd found my way home. And once back in the Underlibrary, I was quickly able to work out whom I had encountered. It also put his mutterings about a child who had ruined his plans into context."

Melville looked at Tilly. "Which brings me to the next item on my agenda. I have become increasingly concerned about the effects that children have on the security of bookwandering. The exploits of your granddaughter—and her friend—do nothing to change my mind. I plan to limit bookwandering for under-eighteens until they can learn discipline, not to mention learn the history and traditions of our great institution."

"You can't stop us from bookwandering!" Tilly said in horror.

"That's barbaric," Grandma said. "Why would you want to cut children off from the magic and wonder of bookwandering?"

"Because they do not have enough respect for the rules, and because bookwandering is about more than *magic* and *wonder*," he said, managing to imbue those words with pure disdain.

"Anyway, regardless of your shoddy logic, it's not possible to stop someone from bookwandering," Grandad said. "As you well know."

"We may not be able to stifle someone's natural ability," Melville said calmly. "But we can certainly bind the books here at the Underlibrary and restrict access."

"But a book doesn't know how old a reader or wanderer is," Grandad said. "There's no way of putting an age limit on it."

"You're right," Melville said. "So I imagine we shall have to bind the books for everyone and require people to file written permission to access them for bookwandering purposes. That's a neat solution, don't you think? We can ensure people are only bookwandering with valid reasons, not merely for a jaunt, or to cause mischief. Or indeed to seduce a fictional character." He raised an eyebrow.

"How dare you make such crass implications about my daughter?" Grandma said, and Tilly felt her hands squeeze involuntarily into fists, her fingernails pushing painfully into her palms.

"That's not fair!" Tilly burst out. "That's not what happened at all!"

"I suggest you control yourself," Melville said. "Your outburst only supports my position."

"Do you know, you sound an awful lot like Enoch Chalk?" Grandma said coldly, and Melville let annoyance cross his face for a moment.

"I can assure you that I am the very opposite," Melville said. "Not that I have to justify myself to you. As you saw just minutes ago, the librarians are on my side. And one more thing. In the meantime, I think it's probably wise to introduce a period of stamping, so we can keep track of everyone's whereabouts."

"But that's a gross invasion of privacy," Grandma said, and Tilly felt cold all over at the memory of Chalk stamping her without her knowledge so he could try to find out who her parents were.

"Anyway, no one will agree," Grandad said. "Everyone will opt out."

"On the contrary, it's already been agreed to. It's now mandatory to opt in."

"Mandatory opt-in?" Grandad snorted. "A complete oxymoron. You can't just change the meanings of words at your own will."

"On the contrary," Melville said. "Words can mean much more, or less, than they seem, and we can put them to such creative uses. The majority of our librarians understand, or are being made to understand, that stamping is for the best at this time of uncertainty. After all, if you're not going anywhere you're not supposed to, you shouldn't have any concerns, should you? It would look awfully suspicious if you didn't want your fellow bookwanderers to know where you were going. And before you get on your high horse, remember stamping only traces which books you're traveling inside. No one will be watching your every move in your day-to-day life, or anything sinister like that. Come now, we're librarians after all. Seb will take you to be registered. Thank you for your cooperation. It's an exciting time for British bookwandering. You are honored to be witnessing it."

"Hang on—" Oskar started to say, but Melville interrupted him.

"That's all for now. Thank you for your time."

"You won't get away with this," Grandad said to Melville.

"And yet, I seem to be doing just that," Melville said, not looking up.

7

Book Magic

As soon as the door was closed behind them, Grandad went to speak, but Seb glared at him and put a finger to his own lips.

"Wait until we're somewhere private," he whispered urgently, and so they walked in a silent line into another office, this one much more sparsely decorated than the last.

"I refuse to be stamped!" Grandad said as soon as the door was closed. "It's an obvious and egregious infringement of my rights as a person and a bookwanderer. The Underlibrary has no legal right to do anything to us."

"No, of course not," Seb said. "But it does have powers over bookwandering, and it is within its rights—if on dubious ethical grounds—to say, for example, that only stamped bookwanderers are permitted to wander within books under the jurisdiction of the British Underlibrary. You know a stamp isn't permanent—Tilly isn't still stamped from when Chalk was following her." Tilly shuddered at the memory.

"Come on, Seb, you don't need to do this," Grandma said.

"I would never even think of it," Seb said, affronted. "But it's not me who's doing it. I only found out this was the plan during the Inking Ceremony when my friend Willow warned me. Amelia thinks that I should ingratiate myself with Melville, so I can report back. But I don't think he's convinced of my allegiance yet, and he's sending along someone else to do the stamping so I can't sneak you out. The only thing that I can think of is to—" At that moment the door banged open and a petite woman walked in.

"I'll take over from here, Sebastian," she said formally.

"Of course, Angelica," he said. "I'll just take Tilly and Oskar next door."

"Why?" she said, frowning.

"Didn't Mr. Underwood tell you? Because of his new guidelines for child bookwanderers, they're being stamped by Willow a few doors down, so there's a separate record for under-eighteens. Surely . . . Melville told you, didn't he? How embarrassing if I've spilled the beans before I was supposed to."

"Of course not," Angelica said, blustering. "I knew that—I was just checking you did. I'm actually rather in the inner circle nowadays," she said, smiling smugly.

"Yes, yes," Seb said, ushering Tilly and Oskar out of the door. "Well done, very important, I'm sure. I'll take them in. How long do you need?"

"Only ten minutes or so," she said.

"What about Grandma and Grandad?" Tilly hissed at him as Seb shoved her and Oskar into an empty room.

"I am sure they will think of something," he said. "If it came down to it, I'm sure they would prefer to make sure you don't get stamped. They're more than capable of fending for themselves."

"Can Underwood check if we've been stamped, though?" Oskar asked Seb nervously.

"Well, he can check the record, yes," Seb said. "And I will duly be writing your names down so they appear to be there. And if he checks the stamp to see where you've been, then it won't show any record of bookwandering."

"How does he check?" Oskar asked.

"The stamps are linked to what ends up looking a lot like a diary," Seb explained. "Where you've bookwandered will be recorded in a list showing when and where you went. Yours will stay blank because you're not actually being stamped—but he'll assume that he has frightened you into submission. Showing that he does not know you very well, I might add."

"Couldn't you do that for my grandparents as well?" Tilly said.

"I think Melville would be more suspicious if they were showing as not bookwandering at all. There's no chance he would think he could scare Archie and Elsie."

And despite how worried she felt, Tilly couldn't help but feel a little proud.

"So what is it that Angelica is actually going to do to them?" Oskar said. "Tilly didn't realize when she'd been stamped, so it's obviously not, like, a big ink stamp . . . is it?"

"No, not quite so literal," Seb said, smiling despite the situation. "Chalk must have secretly stamped Tilly that first time he visited Pages & Co. To put a library stamp on someone, you just need to get a little bit of book magic to stick to them, and then you can trace that magic trail. As Melville said, it doesn't tell anyone where you are in real life; it simply creates a sort of diary, or map, of the books you've wandered into. It's not harmful, but Melville's plan to use so much book magic is deeply concerning. This magic is woven into the structure of stories, but extracting it is a violent thing. You have to break a story a little bit, cause a rupture, and then you can siphon off some of that book's magic. In the Underlibrary, our main source, when and if we need it, is from books that are out of print or that have a major error in them and can't be sold or loaned. We buy them up and pulp them, and can distill a little bit of book magic from them. Our method may not extract such potent magic, but it doesn't endanger stories in the same way. Remember, books are just the holders of stories, not the thing itself. And so, if someone wants to be traced—say if they are going into a dangerous book—they can wear a little bit of book magic in a locket, or simply dab a bit onto their body. It looks a lot like ink. In fact, as you saw at the Ceremony earlier, the ink used there has book magic in it to bind the Librarians to the Underlibrary and vice versa."

"How long does it last?" Oskar asked.

"If you put book magic directly on your skin, it lasts a few months at most," Seb said. "And that's the other reason we don't need to worry too much about your grandparents. They just need to be careful for a bit, while we work out a proper plan."

"Okay," Tilly said, feeling a little calmer. "You know, when people talked about book magic, I didn't realize they were talking about a physical thing."

"Same," Oskar said. "I thought it was all, like, ooooh, the magic of books! Reading is important! You know, like teachers say."

"Oh no," Seb said. "I mean, what teachers say is of course true, but our book magic is what runs through all stories and powers them. Did you hear what Melville said about fairy tales? They're so unstable because they're running on pure book magic that's not contained in Source Editions and printed books. It's ancient book magic—even Librarians don't really understand how it works."

"But, Seb, hang on," Tilly started. "What did Melville mean when he talked about binding all the books? Does that use book magic too?"

"Well, as Mr. Underwood said, it's not possible to take

someone's bookwandering abilities away from them—they're a part of you. But you can stop people from accessing certain books. If a Source Edition of a book is 'bound,' then no one can wander inside any of the versions of it. It controls where people can wander. There was a group of bookwanderers back in the early nineteenth century who thought that bookwandering should be limited to only certain types of people—rich like them, mainly. Now there are some Librarians here who have taken their name, the 'Bookbinders,' and are spouting nonsense about control being a good thing."

"But why?" Tilly asked. "What's in it for them?"

"Power, mainly," Seb said. "If you control something, it gives you power over the people who want it—or need it. People like the Bookbinders hate the idea of something being shared out and enjoyed. They think they deserve to have it all to themselves. And so it has always been."

"But just because something has always been that way doesn't make it right," Tilly said.

"Of course not," Seb said. "But it does make it difficult to change. It doesn't mean we shouldn't try, though."

"Seb," Tilly said. "Do you think Melville really has found Chalk?"

"It would seem so," Seb said. "And that's a good thing, even if we don't agree with anything else he's doing. Bookwandering is complicated; it's not as easy as people who aren't for us being against us."

"I think it's clear he is *definitely* against us," Oskar said. "Not sure that's too complicated."

"But that doesn't mean we don't want some things in common," Seb said. "Such as finding Chalk. It's in no one's interest for Chalk to roam around stories, especially fairy tales. So let's focus our energies on stopping Melville's bigger bookbinding plans, and let him deal with Chalk."

At that moment, they heard a door being slammed shut, and they poked their heads out of the room to see three very angry, flustered-looking people glaring at each other in the corridor.

"I'm just doing my job, Mr. Pages," Angelica was saying. "I didn't make this decision. And now I'm leaving. Take it up with Mr. Underwood if you're unhappy."

"Have you considered maybe thinking for yourself for one moment?" Grandad said crossly. "You don't have to do everything you're told."

"The thing is," Grandma said, clearly making a conscious effort to remain calm, "it's important to think about what you're being asked to do, and whether you think it's right."

"This isn't something I want to lose my job over," Angelica said. "Isn't the whole point of the senior librarians to worry about this sort of thing for us, so we don't have to?"

"No!" Grandad exploded. "Their purpose is to protect bookwandering! Not to be blustering, idiotic tyrants!" He noticed the others, peering through the door behind him. "Finally! Tilly,

Oskar, let's go. I do not want to stay one more moment in an institution that has become the very antithesis of what it was set up to do!" He took Tilly and Oskar by the shoulder and steered them out of the door, Grandma and Seb following.

"To the Map Room, yes?" Grandad said. "We need to get back to Pages & Co. as quickly as possible."

"Do you think that's wise?" Seb said nervously.

"I could not care less at this point," Grandad replied. "Could you please tell Amelia to get in touch with us as soon as she is able to extricate herself from this place?"

"Yes, of course," Seb said. "And don't worry about Tilly and Oskar," he added. "I didn't stamp them."

Grandad softened. "Thank you, Seb," he said. "I should never have doubted you. Please come and see us with Amelia if you can. There is a lot to talk about."

8

What an Adventure

Half an hour later they were sitting around the kitchen table drinking very strong cups of tea with out-of-character two spoons of sugar, or usually-reserved-for-special-occasions fizzy drinks.

"I'm still not sure I understand how we can travel from the Map Room home," Tilly said. "Is it book magic too? And can we get to the Underlibrary the same way?"

"Ah," Grandad said, a little sheepishly. "Well, yes and no. It's not exactly an approved transport method. And Pages & Co. shouldn't technically still be on the network."

"When you're the Librarian," Grandma explained, "you get a few favors from some of our fictional friends. One of those is that a character who specializes in magical doors and portals, say a charismatic lion or similar, will come and create one in the Underlibrary Map Room that opens in the Librarian's home bookshop or library—just in case of emergencies. It's supposed to be closed when a new Librarian takes over, so we don't have magic portals crisscrossing the country. Not to mention it's generally frowned upon to bring magical characters into the real world. But Amelia turned a blind eye when she took over, and I think we can assume that she won't be letting Melville know that the Pages & Co. portal still exists."

"In case you need to get back in without him noticing?" Oskar asked.

"Precisely," Grandad said.

"Although let's hope it doesn't come to that," Grandma said. "We need to understand a lot more about what exactly is going on before we start sneaking around."

"So . . . what do we do first?" Tilly asked.

"Well, you two are doing exactly what you were always going to do." Grandma smiled. "You're going to Paris tomorrow morning to visit Oskar's dad for Christmas!"

"But what about Melville and the stamping and the bookbinding? And banning children from bookwandering! Can't I help?" Tilly persisted.

"While you're away, we will speak to Amelia and Seb properly," Grandma replied. "In hindsight, it perhaps wasn't such a good idea for you both to come today, but thankfully Seb has diverted any immediate problems—*not* that this is permission for you to bookwander anywhere dangerous, of course."

"And don't worry about us," said Grandad. "The stamping

is an ethical problem, not a practical one. It will wear off soon and it's not like we had any illicit bookwandering trips planned. The thing we need to focus on is stopping them from binding books, and you can leave that to us. We'll talk to some librarians about the Bookbinders. And, of course, leave Chalk to Melville."

"Is there really nothing we can do to help?" Oskar asked.

"Not right now," Grandad said.

"Not even any research or reading or anything?" Tilly persisted.

"You can help by having a wonderful time in Paris meeting Oskar's dad," Grandad said firmly. "Leave this one to us. And now, dinner!"

Half an hour later Grandad set down a big bowl full of spaghetti cooked with tomatoes and prawns. Grandma added hot buttery garlic bread and an arugula salad as Bea came and joined them from the just-closed bookshop. The table bore the marks and memories of years of the Pages family; the underside was still covered with the remnants of Tilly's attempt to turn it into a spaceship when she was younger, sticking colored paper buttons on with superglue. The surface had several red wine stains, a collection of pale circles where hot drinks had been put down without coasters, and copious scratches on the legs from Alice the cat. It held center stage in the area that functioned as a dining room, a study, and a private family space away from the bookshop. It was rare for the table not to be covered with piles of books, half-done homework, lukewarm cups of tea, or unopened mail.

"So, Oskar," Grandma said, sitting down. "How long has it been since you've been to Paris?" Oskar was busy trying to sneak a corner of garlic bread into his mouth, before realizing quite how hot it was.

"I haven't been since the summer holidays," Oskar said, trying to suck cool air into his mouth as he replied. "With Mamie sick over half-term, and school and stuff . . . You know how busy everything gets. And Dad hardly gets any holiday, so he can't come here very often either."

"It's very kind of your dad to invite Tilly as well," Bea said, twirling her fork around her pasta without ever raising it to her mouth. "What did you say his job was?"

"He runs an art gallery with my stepmum," Oskar said. "They're super-busy all the time. I think it was Mum's idea for us to go, probably."

"They do know I'm coming, though, right?" Tilly said, alarmed.

"Yes, of course," Grandma reassured her. "We've spoken to him several times on the phone to sort out train tickets and what you need to take—they're really looking forward to meeting you. And you'll get to meet Oskar's grandmother, too, as she's staying with them—maybe you'll even see some of her illustrations!"

"There's one of her paintings up in my dad's place," Oskar confirmed. "It's super-creepy and cool."

"What a treat," Grandma said, trying to coax some enthusiasm out of Tilly.

"It's going to be strange not being at Pages & Co. just before Christmas," was all Tilly said.

"But what an adventure!" Grandad said. "Being in Paris at Christmastime!"

"We'll miss you a lot, though, won't we, Bea?" Grandma said, nudging her daughter.

"I can barely remember what Christmas is like," Bea said, almost to herself. "It will be curious having a tree and turkey and all of that again."

"Didn't you have Christmas in *A Little Princess*?" Oskar asked.

"Well, I assume we must have," Bea said slowly. "But I find it hard to remember anything specific about being there at all, really. It's like trying to remember a dream. I just can't seem to picture any of it." And she went back to toying with her wineglass.

Tilly had hoped that her mum would settle back into normal life more each day, following her rescue from *A Little Princess*. But the opposite seemed to be true. Bea spent more and more time by herself, and could be found lost in her own daydreams for much of the day. Pushing her glass to one side, Bea shook her head and smiled—properly—at Tilly.

"But you'll only be gone for a couple of days, and you'll be back in plenty of time for Christmas. Now, who's up for coffee?"

Bea moved her nearly full bowl away from her and stood up, mussing Tilly's hair as she went to put the kettle on. Tilly tried to shove away her worries about her mother into a room right at the very back of her brain—along with her worries about what was going on at the Underlibrary. She wedged a chair under the door handle for good measure, to keep them locked in tight.

9

Something Wild and Beautiful

There was something special about Pages & Co. first thing in the morning, especially if you were the only one in the shop. There was an air of expectation and endless possibility stacked neatly along the tidy shelves, adventure tucked between dust jackets. Tilly sat cross-legged on the emerald-green velvet sofa by the fireplace and watched the snow fall outside. The shop was still chilly, and Tilly's hands were wrapped around a hot cup of a homemade concoction that Grandma called mulled Ribena. She sipped carefully as the snowflakes danced and settled on the glass.

"I sometimes imagine they are tiny dancing snow sprites," a familiar voice said, and Tilly turned to see Anne Shirley, the heroine of one of Tilly's favorite books, sitting at the other end of the sofa staring out of the window in wonder.

"Oh!" Tilly said abruptly, looking at her. "Anne . . . do you know that your hair is green?"

Anne turned and looked at her mournfully.

"I have had such a terrible time of it. You would scarcely believe it could all happen to one person," she said dejectedly. "Truly the fates are against me. I thought I was dyeing it a beautiful, elegant raven black, but the man I bought the dye from at the doorstep has cruelly taken advantage of my vanity and, well, look. I have been washing it furiously for three days straight now and no change. My life in the most glittering of social circles has ended before it had a chance to even begin. It is one thing to go to a dance as a redhead, but quite another to make an entrance with green hair, especially in a town so ravenous for gossip as Avonlea. Just imagine what Rachel Lynde would say if she saw me!" She flopped her head dramatically onto the back of the sofa and let out a groan of woe. "I am far too embarrassed to leave Green Gables—I will only permit dear Diana to visit, as she is able to behave in the somber manner that befits the situation—and so it's a pleasant surprise to find myself here. Were you thinking of me?"

"I suppose I must have been in some way, for you to arrive," Tilly said. "And do you know, short hair is very fashionable here? You could always cut it."

"Oh, I don't think so," Anne said solemnly. "Why, the only thing worse than green hair would be short green hair. And if it comes to that, I think I shall have to withdraw from polite society entirely."

"Well, fingers crossed it doesn't come to that," Tilly said weakly, knowing—from having reread *Anne of Green Gables* just the other week—that it was destined to turn out exactly like that. Anne rested her green head on Tilly's shoulder and sighed.

"Winter is the most magical time of year, isn't it?"

"You say that about every season," Tilly said affectionately.

"Perhaps," Anne said. "But the important thing is that I mean it fiercely in the moment. I do sometimes find that I mean things wholly and entirely when I say them only to discover that the next day, or the next season, my opinions have changed. Marilla says this makes no matter, and that falsehoods dressed up as enthusiasm are still falsehoods, but I think that if you mean something sincerely when you say it, then it is the truth, whatever happens next, and that enthusiasm is a very good reason for almost anything—especially winter."

"I wonder what winter in Paris will be like," Tilly mused.

"You're going to Paris?" Anne said, sitting bolt upright. "Why, how perfectly romantic! When are you going?"

"Very soon," Tilly said. "Our train leaves St. Pancras station just before lunchtime, I think. Although I'm not sure it's a good time to be going. . . ."

"Whyever not?" Anne asked. "I should have thought that there was no such thing as a bad time to go to Paris!"

"Well, a lot has been going on here," Tilly said. "And I don't really know where I fit into it all. Grandma and Grandad say they're going to fix everything while we're away, but I don't really see how they will be able to do that, and Amelia—our friend—has lost her job, and no one seems worried about what Chalk is up to. And I just don't know what anything means, and it feels strange to just pop over to Paris for a holiday when everyone seems so stressed and my mum is still so sad."

"She's still sad?" Anne asked gently.

"Yes," Tilly said. "And she basically stays here all the time. She hasn't gone into any stories since we said good-bye to my dad, and she won't even talk to me about it either. It's like we're strangers."

"Well, it must be ever so peculiar to go from having a newborn daughter one day and then, suddenly, the next time you see her, she's eleven and a whole proper person with her own dreams and memories and desires," Anne said. "It's one of those ideas that sounds like it might be quite romantic if you read it in a book, but when it happens to one of your bosom friends, you can't help but worry it's a little confusing and tragic."

"I mean, I'm not sure I'd go quite as far as tragic," Tilly said, bristling. "At least she's back now. You shouldn't feel sorry for me."

"I don't at all," Anne said earnestly. "How could I feel sorry for someone who lives in a bookshop and has two grandparents, and one whole mother to love her, and is going to Paris in the snow! Why, I would never trade Green Gables for anything, but I would not be so sad to have your lot in life."

"I suppose so," Tilly said, trying to feel as lucky as she knew she was, really.

The sound of the kitchen door banging made her jump, and she looked up to see Grandma heading her way.

"Are you all right, love?" she asked, sitting next to Tilly on the sofa, a book under one arm.

"Anne's just gone," Tilly said. "We were just chatting. And she had green hair."

"Ah, the green hair incident. I wish I could have seen it. It's good to have friends you can talk things through with, you know," Grandma said. "I'm glad you have Anne, and Oskar. He takes in more than I think you sometimes realize. It will be lovely for you both to visit Paris and his family. Now, I wanted to share something with you before you go."

Grandma placed the book she was carrying gently on her lap. "I thought you might like to have a look at this—it's my book of fairy tales back from when I was working in the Underlibrary—it's where I used to start from when I was mapping them."

The book was very old and battered, with slips of paper marking certain yellowed pages and a few corners turned down. Tilly carefully opened the front cover and saw an intricately decorated contents page of familiar stories.

"France is in some ways the home of fairy tales, certainly those in the Western tradition that are most familiar to us. Many of them were first written down in France, even if they originated elsewhere," Grandma explained. "It's too dangerous to bookwander there at the moment, but if you fancy it, maybe we could go together once everything's settled down?"

"Yes, please," Tilly said as she turned through the pages. "You said . . . You said there was a difference of opinion and that's why you stopped working in fairy tales?"

"Well, yes," Grandma said, a little hesitantly. "When I was the Cartographer, I worked with another librarian, who used to be a close friend, and our job was to try to create a map of how fairy tales fit together, and to research why the usual rules don't apply there. We wandered together many times, exploring the stories and the fairy-tale lands. It really is a fas-cinating place. But once we started to get somewhere with our research, the next stage was to use what we'd learned to make fairy tales safer for bookwanderers, and to share our maps. However, my friend got what I can only describe as cold feet about the whole project. Through our time inside the stories, she decided that we shouldn't be trying to make them safer, and their danger was what made them special. She believed that we were trying to impose order on something wild and beautiful. And to be honest, I agree with her to a certain point, but she started seeing conspiracy theories everywhere and ended up being forced to . . . Well, she ended up leaving the Underlibrary."

"Why does nobody seem to be able to agree on how book-wandering should work?" Tilly asked.

"Well, it's all very complicated, more so than you realize," Grandma said. "Sometimes I feel that we should do away with the Underlibrary altogether and let people just wander as they like, but then I think about Bea falling in love with your father and wanting to stay in *A Little Princess*, and then I think we need some rules and organization. I'm not sure we'll ever know the right answers to every question. We're all just doing our best."

"Mr. Underwood isn't," Tilly said firmly.

"Well, no," Grandma admitted. "What he's doing isn't for the best, I don't think. But I am sure he believes it is. And if you can understand why someone is doing something, it's always a good start, even if you want to stop them. You heard what Amelia said: there's something going on behind the scenes here, something motivating Melville Underwood beyond mere power. We'll discuss it with Amelia and Seb and see what we can uncover."

"And what about Chalk?" Tilly said. "He's just getting away with what he did to Mum. Don't you think he should be punished in some way?"

"Do you?" Grandma asked.

"Yes!" Tilly said. "It's not fair, otherwise."

"Well, I am sure that Melville is trying to find him and bring him to justice—whatever that might mean," Grandma said. "Melville is a very clever man, regardless of any of his less appealing characteristics, and getting Chalk back into his own story would be excellent for his reputation. I imagine Melville would love to have that success to mark the beginning of his career as Librarian. Chalk can't cause any damage to our family, wherever he is, and you'll be safe in Paris, away from this for a while. Don't do any bookwandering, just to be on the safe side, and you'll be back here before you know it."

"What do you mean, don't do any bookwandering?" Tilly asked, shocked. "None at all?"

Grandma frowned. "Surely you see that given the situation it's best that you don't go into any books while you're far from home?"

"I thought you said that Chalk couldn't hurt us?" Tilly said.

"Well, no," Grandma said. "But it's a time to stay safe, Tilly—and stay away from any regular bookwandering dangers. It's only for a short time, while everything settles down. Now, you'd better check you have everything for your trip."

Grandma stood up, and left the book of fairy tales on the sofa. And a few minutes later Tilly slipped it inside her backpack that was waiting by the door. If people were going to keep secrets from her, then she was going to do a little research of her own.

Grandad was talking through the arrangements for meeting Oskar's father, Gabriel, at the other end, for what felt like the tenth time that morning, before the taxi arrived to take them to St. Pancras station to catch the Eurostar.

"We'll be fine," Tilly said, wanting to stop talking about leaving and get on with it. "How much can go wrong on a train in two and a half hours?"

Grandad raised an eyebrow. "I've seen you two make more mischief in ten minutes than most people could make in a lifetime."

"Fair," Oskar said, sounding quite proud.

"Is Mum coming to say good-bye?" Tilly asked quietly.

"Ah, my love, I don't think so," Grandad said. "You know how tired she gets since she got back. You said good-bye last night, didn't you?"

Tilly shrugged helplessly. A good-bye last night didn't make it better that her own mother hadn't bothered to come downstairs to see her off.

"You'll be back before you know it," Grandad said, picking up the bags. "And we've got a proper Pages & Co. Christmas planned for when you're home. You and your mum can speak all the time while you're away—I know she'll want to talk to you every day and hear about what you're up to."

Tilly didn't say anything, but picked up her bag and went

outside to the waiting car. Then, just as she was settling into her seat, the bookshop door swung open and Bea rushed out, snuggled into a fleecy blue robe and flannel pajamas.

"Tilly," she said, sounding slightly out of breath. "I'm so glad I caught you." She stopped and looked at Tilly, and the delicate, precious thread of their relationship hung between them. "I'm going to miss you," Bea said, and wrapped her up in a huge, self-conscious hug. "Happy Christmas," she whispered into Tilly's ear. "I love you very much."

Tilly's heart instantly felt lighter, and she happily waved at her mum out of the taxi window, until she was just a fuzzy shape on the horizon, waving in the middle of the road.

10

A Deep, Dark Forest

The taxi pulled up at St. Pancras station, and Tilly, Oskar, and Grandad walked through the airy glass-ceilinged building that echoed with someone bashing out Christmas carols on a slightly out-of-tune public piano. They made their way through throngs of Tube-map-clutching tourists and festive travelers to the busy lines at the Eurostar entrance. Grandad helped them find their seats on the train, and tracked down the steward tasked with keeping an eye on Tilly and Oskar on the journey to Paris. After a good five minutes of fussing and checking to make sure they were still in possession of the various documents, currencies, and phone numbers they needed, the steward intervened and took Grandad gently by the elbow.

"Sir, the train needs to leave now," he said, closing the door firmly. "I promise we'll take good care of them." And with a train whistle and a last wave to Grandad, they were on their way.

"Do you mind if I read?" Tilly asked straightaway, pulling Grandma's stolen—or secretly borrowed, as Tilly preferred to think of it—fairy-tale book out of her backpack.

"Oh. Sure," Oskar said. "Cool. I might go and explore, see if there's a café. Do you want anything?"

"I'm okay, thank you," Tilly said, without looking up. Oskar shrugged and set off, wobbling along the aisle with the rhythm of the moving train.

Tilly ran a careful finger down the contents page, keeping an eye out for anything that might tell her a little more about Grandma as a young woman mapping fairy tales. But there was nothing written in the book, and none of the slips of paper functioning as bookmarks said anything on them. With nothing else to go on, she chose a story marked with a page corner turned down, and settled back in her seat to read. It was "Little Red Riding Hood" and Tilly was on high alert for anything that seemed different from how she remembered the story, when a

strange, sticky, sweet
smell wafted toward her.
Assuming it was Oskar back
with some snacks, she glanced
up, but he was nowhere to be seen.

She looked around, searching for the source
of the smell, and was surprised to see, through
the window, that the train was running through a
deep, dark forest. Tilly was sure that there weren't any
forests of this size within a twenty-minute train ride of
north London, and yet there it was. The trees seemed
to crowd in on every side, as if they were trying
to reach inside the train with their spindly
branches.

Tilly sat back, confused. She put the book on the table in front of her and bent down to fish her phone out of her bag so she could look at the maps app, but an insistent tapping noise startled her. She sat upright and saw

trees pressing in unnaturally closely, their branches and leaves scratching and scraping at the windows as the train rushed by. Tilly looked around, searching for signs of worry among the other passengers, but

everyone else was absorbed in their phones
or books, or snoozing. Her breathing started to
quicken in panic as the **darkness closed in,**
casting the whole train into **shadow,**
and yet still no one else seemed to react. A cracking noise
like boots on a frozen lake echoed in Tilly's ears, and she
shrank back as a tree branch that suddenly seemed conscious and full of intent snaked its way through the
window, as if the glass just wasn't there, and curled

its way up and across the ceiling of the train. More and more branches followed it, filling the train with treacherous ropes of bark. Leaves thrashed in the air as if caught in a hurricane. Tilly watched in terror as a sinuous branch crept under her feet and across the aisle toward an elderly man sleeping with his mouth slightly ajar. It slithered up his side and across his eyes, and Tilly felt as though she were trapped inside a horror film as the branch seemed to be making for his open mouth.

"Stop!" she shouted, panicked. "Wake up!" She flung herself across the seats and onto the sleeping man, trying to grab at the branch before it suffocated him.

"What on earth do you think you're doing?" he spluttered, self-consciously wiping drool from the corner of his mouth.

"I was stopping the trees!" she said, but the moment the words were out of her mouth, the trees were nowhere to be seen. They had simply vanished, and wintery sun was spilling through the windows. The man was looking at her with concern.

"What trees?" he said. "Are your parents around?"

"I'm so sorry," Tilly said, face burning with embarrassment, as she retreated across the aisle to her seat. "I just thought . . . I just saw . . . I'm so sorry; please just pretend I didn't do that."

The man glanced around, looking for parents, or a guard, but evidently decided it wasn't worth the effort of complaining about her to someone.

"Just stay in your seat," he said sternly, before leaning his head back and promptly falling asleep again.

Tilly pressed her face against the window, trying to catch a glimpse of the forest, but it was nowhere to be seen. Her tummy did a flip-flop of nervousness. She knew enough to realize that whatever it was she had just seen, it was not supposed to have happened.

"Hey, you dropped this," Oskar said, reaching down and picking up Grandma's fairy-tale book, which had fallen awkwardly on the train floor in Tilly's panic, crushing the page she had been reading. She turned it over, trying to smooth the page down and went pale as she noticed what was on the other side. An intricate black-and-white drawing of a deep, dark forest teased at the edges of the picture, as if it were trying to escape.

Oskar laid out a carton of orange juice and a greasy cardboard sleeve containing a microwaved cheese sandwich cut in half. "I thought we could share," he said, pushing half of the sandwich toward Tilly. "I got an extra straw for the juice too. Hey." He looked at her closely. "Are you okay? You look really pale—are you motion sick? Do you want some water instead?"

"No, I'm fine, thank you," Tilly said, not quite ready to share with Oskar what had happened. She was tired of always having strange, confusing things happen to her, and for once she didn't want to think about it at all. She gingerly picked up the sandwich, trying to avoid burning her fingers on the cheese. "I just thought I saw something weird out the window, but it was a trick of the light, I guess."

"Okay," Oskar said, sounding unconvinced as he poked

two straws through the top of the juice carton. "Hang on." He reached forward and picked something out of Tilly's bangs. "You've got a leaf in your hair!"

"Weird," Tilly said, trying to sound surprised as she took the dry leaf from Oskar's hand and crumbled it under her fingers.

Two and a half hours later, the Eurostar pulled into the Gare du Nord in Paris. Tilly and Oskar dragged their cases out onto a platform in a large station full of intricate green ironwork.

"There!" Oskar shouted, elbowing Tilly harder than he had meant to. He pointed at a man standing at the other end of the platform. "Let's go!"

When the man spotted them, his face broke into a wide grin and he met them halfway down the platform, scooping Oskar up into a bear hug.

"And you must be Matilda," he said in perfect English with a broad French accent. He was a tall man with dark hair and stubble, wearing slim-cut pants and oxfords, and an elegant black coat. "I am Oskar's father, Gabriel."

"Hi," Tilly said, feeling overwhelmingly shy. "I'm Tilly, really, not Matilda. Well, I am Matilda. But everyone calls me Tilly."

"Welcome, Tilly," Gabriel said, smiling. "We are so glad you are here."

"Thank you for having me," she said politely.

"It's our absolute pleasure," Gabriel said. "It's so wonderful you could come with Oskar—he and Mary both talk about you so much. Let's get you home and have some lunch. *On y va!*"

They traveled via the Paris Métro, which was nearly but not quite like the London Underground, to a stop only fifteen minutes away. There they climbed up a steep set of stairs and emerged onto the streets of Paris, which curled around Tilly like something out of a story themselves, all frost and magic and romance. They were standing on a narrow street resting under a fine layer of snow, and the air was prickly fresh around them. A green metal sign arched over their heads with the name of the station in elaborate black writing, and cafés squeezed up next to each other along the other side of the road. Despite the cold, several of them still had chairs and tables on the street hiding under snow-laden striped canopies, and an elegant French couple sat drinking hot chocolate outside one of them.

They followed the narrow road to its end and turned into a small, frosty square. Pale stone buildings were wrapped with dark vines that would turn into purple wisteria in the summer. They headed toward one corner of the square and to a big old-fashioned wooden door that opened onto a flight of stone steps.

"No lift, I'm afraid," Gabriel said. "But we're only on the second floor, so not too bad. Welcome, Tilly, and welcome home, Oskar—let's go inside and get warm."

They climbed the stairs to a periwinkle-blue door that opened off a small landing. As Gabriel opened the door the delicious smell of festive spices of nutmeg and clove filled the air, and behind that was the distinct pine-smell of a real Christmas tree. Tilly could hear Handel's *Messiah* playing from another room as Gabriel ushered them in.

"Come in, come in," Oskar said excitedly, leading her through the corridor and depositing his shoes on top of an existing heap underneath a mirror. Tilly copied him, trying to add her shoes sort of neatly, and Gabriel took her coat and scarf, hanging them on two of a series of hooks on the opposite wall.

"Welcome, welcome!" a voice said, and a petite woman with a broad smile appeared from a door. "Oskar, look how much you've grown!" she said, giving him a hug. "And this must be Matilda! It is wonderful to meet you; thank you for coming to stay with us. I am Marguerite, Gabriel's wife." She leaned forward and kissed Tilly on both cheeks. She smelled like fancy perfume.

"Thank you for having me," Tilly said. "You can call me Tilly."

"Tilly! How lovely! Now come in out of the corridor. We'll take your bags up and show you your room once you've warmed up and had some lunch."

The three of them followed Marguerite into the high-ceilinged living room, which was a cacophony of colors and textures. The space was dominated by large windows that looked out over Paris, and there were two chairs under the window with colorful blankets draped over their backs. A Christmas tree was squeezed into one corner, decorated entirely with white fairy lights and silver decorations, and the source of the classical music Tilly had heard was revealed to be a record player perched on top of a cabinet full of vinyl records.

They went through to the kitchen, which had another tall window that would open out onto a tiny balcony when the weather was sunnier. There was a wooden table pushed against the opposite wall, piled with food—a fresh baguette generously sliced, a plate with three different kinds of cheeses, a big patterned bowl full of salad leaves, and a matching smaller bowl heaped with green and black olives. As they all settled down for lunch, talking of trains and cheese and Christmas, Tilly thought how nice it would be to have two days without any bookwandering or bookbinding or any kind of book magic at all.

11

What's the Worst
That Could Happen?

"...And that is why you should never trust a sheep farmer
from Marseille," Gabriel finished triumphantly, at
the end of a very long and confusing story about
dairy farming in France. "But enough about cheese. Let me
show you two where you're sleeping. I'll save my brie facts for
tomorrow."

Tilly tried to smile and nod politely. She had never heard
anyone talk about cheese for such a long time. Gabriel picked
up their suitcases from the corridor and pointed at two closed
doors. "That one's the bathroom." He gestured. "And that one is
usually the study, but it's where my mother is staying, recuperat-
ing from her operation. She is currently sleeping. I am sure she'll
say hello shortly."

Tilly and Oskar followed Gabriel up the narrow staircase to
Oskar's older sister's room, where Tilly would be sleeping. It was
a small, square space with fairy lights dipped from one corner to

another, illuminating posters and magazine cuttings about philosophy, feminism, and poetry. Two large, messy bookcases took up most of one wall, and a huge poster of Simone de Beauvoir hung over a bed heaped with blankets. Tilly was a little disappointed she couldn't see the Eiffel Tower from the apartment, but she supposed that was like coming to London and expecting to see Big Ben out of every window.

"We should have a look through Emilie's books," Oskar said once Gabriel had left. "See if there's anything we can bookwander inside!"

"No," Tilly said, trying to push whatever had happened on the train out of her mind. "We can't do it from here, remember? You can only bookwander from a bookshop or a library. Anyway, Grandma told me not to, just in case."

"Oh, come on," Oskar said. "It's not like we're just going to bump into Chalk, is it?"

"Who knows," Tilly said. "All *we* know is that the grown-ups are supposedly going to sort it out. Not that they seem to be doing a very good job of it."

"Who's going to even notice if we bookwander in Paris anyway?" Oskar said, trying to sound persuasive. "We should go somewhere fun and Christmassy! Nowhere dangerous! I bet Mamie knows where the good bookshops are. How about we try to get back to Narnia?"

"Narnia is what you think of as fun and safe and Christmassy?" Tilly said.

"I mean, it's festive, right?" Oskar said. "And fun if we stick to the right bits!"

"I really don't want to meet the White Witch," Tilly said. "And I don't even like Turkish delight."

"You never want to go anywhere exciting," Oskar complained. "We can't just keep going to have picnics with Ratty and Mole in *The Wind in the Willows*, you know."

"Why not?" Tilly said. "It's lovely and funny and, most importantly, safe."

Oskar wasn't letting up. "What's the worst that could happen?"

"You literally had to walk the plank six weeks ago," Tilly pointed out.

"But it worked out fine!"

"And what about everything going on at the Underlibrary!" Tilly said.

"Yeah, but that's just fairy tales, isn't it?" Oskar replied. "I know there's all the bookbinding stuff, but that doesn't make actual bookwandering more dangerous. Books are still safe, and we're not stamped, and do you know, you *could* look at it like we probably ought to do as much bookwandering as possible if Underwood is going to try to stop children at some point in the future . . . ?"

"Okay, that's the first thing you've said that makes sense. But," she said, catching herself, "the point is that Chalk is still out there. We don't know where he's lurking or what he's planning. He could turn any book into a trap!"

"He's stuck in fairy tales if we can believe Underwood," Oskar said. "And anyway, we can't just stop bookwandering altogether. Isn't that what Chalk would want? Isn't that what Underwood wants?"

"I . . . guess," said Tilly hesitantly.

"So we'll just stick together, and always check the last page. Come on, Tilly, we know what we're doing!" Oskar said. "We just avoid fairy tales and we're golden!"

Tilly nodded. "I know, you're right; I just get nervous these days."

"That's okay," Oskar said, smiling mischievously. "We all know you're the sensible, clever one and I'm the exciting, adventurous one."

"Hey!" Tilly protested.

"You're right: I am quite clever too," Oskar said, grinning.

There was a new addition to the living room when they got downstairs. In one of the armchairs under the window, a very petite, very glamorous woman was looking out across the snowy rooftops. Her ice-white hair was piled up into an elegant chignon, and delicate diamond earrings hung from her ears. She was wearing slim-cut black pants, an expensive-looking silky blouse, and a raspberry-pink pashmina that matched her lipstick.

"Mamie!" Oskar said, running over to her and kissing her on both cheeks.

"So formal, *mon cher*," she replied, breaking into a broad smile and gathering him into a gentle hug. "And this must be Matilda!" Tilly hurried over to her chair and stood a little awkwardly in front of her, not sure whether to kiss her or hug her or shake hands. In the end she decided on a quick wave.

"*Bonjour*, uh, *madame*?" she said.

"It is very kind of you to try to speak a little French, Matilda," Mamie said. "But do not worry: I speak English fairly confidently after years working with English writers and publishers. And you may call me Clara."

"You can call me Tilly."

"Wonderful, we are almost friends already, then."

"You worked with English writers?" Tilly asked curiously.

"Why, yes, many of the books I illustrated were English books," Clara said. "If you look behind you, you can see something I drew for a book of fairy tales when I was much younger." Tilly turned to see an intricate watercolor painting of a fairy-tale castle surrounded by a dark forest, all set against a brooding purple sky. She was instantly taken back to the few moments on the train when she had been zipping through a forest just like that one. Tilly found it rather menacing; she could easily imagine all sorts of nightmarish creatures lurking among the trees.

"It's kind of scary," Tilly said, unable to tear her eyes away from it.

"Fairy tales often are," Clara said. "As I am sure you know. I am told you are quite the reader, Tilly. So you must be familiar with the real fairy tales, not just the shiny cartoon versions."

"Yes, I suppose so," Tilly said, still staring into the painted forest, as if she might catch a glimpse of something moving between the tree trunks. "But I never much liked them, to be honest, or not as much as some people do. They're too predictable. Evil stepmothers, witches in disguise. The princess always gets married at the end. The prince always saves her. But I just found out my grandma loves them, so I'm going to give them another try. Maybe I'll like the old ones better."

"I think you might," Clara said. "I wonder if you will find them as predictable as you expect."

"Mamie, we actually wanted to ask you where the nearest bookshop was. We'd love to explore," Oskar said.

"Well, you have many, many to choose from in Paris," Clara said. "But as I imagine you will want something you can read, I would recommend my friend Gretchen's shop, as she has many books in English as well as French. I shall take you there myself tomorrow morning."

"I'm not sure that's wise, Maman," Gabriel said, putting an attentive hand on her shoulder.

"It is really nothing to do with you, *mon cher*," Clara said, gently but firmly removing his hand. "I will order a car to pick us up and to bring me back afterward. It is settled. I am going to retire to the study for now—may I have my dinner in there,

Gabriel?—and I shall see you two at ten o'clock in the morning. *Bonne nuit.*"

And with that she stood up, slowly but gracefully, kissed each of them on the cheek, and left, closing the door behind her.

The rest of the evening was spent chatting and eating, and Tilly felt more at home than she had ever imagined was possible outside of Pages & Co. So much so that it was nearly bedtime when she realized she hadn't spoken to her grandparents, or her mother, since she'd arrived. Tilly excused herself, thanking Gabriel and Marguerite at least three times for having her to stay, and went upstairs to find her phone. There were several missed calls from her grandparents on the screen.

"Hello? Tilly?" Her grandad's urgent voice came over the line. "Are you okay?"

"It's me," Tilly said, feeling guilty. "I'm so sorry I didn't call earlier—everything is fine."

"Okay, darling, but please remember to keep in touch. You feel very far away from us," Grandad said, obviously trying to keep the worry from his voice. "So, what is Oskar's family like?"

"They're lovely," Tilly said. "They've been so welcoming and kind, and we've eaten so much cheese. And I have my own room, and everything is fine, I promise. I've met Clara as well."

"Who's Clara?"

"His grandmother!" Tilly said. "You know, the one who was poorly, the whole reason Oskar was staying over when . . . everything happened."

"Oh! First-name terms already!" Grandad teased, the usual warmth in his voice returning. "I hope you're not in the market for new grandparents already."

"Of course not!" Tilly said. "I'm only interested in grandparents that come ready-made with their own bookshops. And anyway, Clara is kind of . . . I'm not sure what the right word is. She's friendly, but she's also sort of stern. She wears lipstick!"

"I wear lipstick! Sometimes!" Tilly heard her grandmother chime in.

"You're on speakerphone," Grandad explained.

"Is Mum there?" Tilly said.

"I'm here, darling," Bea said. "I'm so glad you're having a nice time already. Is it lovely and festive in Paris? I haven't been since I was a teenager."

"Maybe we should have a family visit next year sometime," Grandma suggested.

"Perhaps," Bea said quietly.

"So what's your plan for tomorrow?" Grandad asked Tilly.

"Clara is taking us to a bookshop," Tilly said. "If that's okay?"

"Of course," Grandad said. "But do be careful, Tilly. We're trusting you and Oskar to be sensible."

Tilly made a noncommittal noise that she hoped conveyed

agreement in a vague sort of way. "Do you think there'll be any bookwanderers at the shop?" she asked.

"I can check for you with Aria in the Map Room," Grandma chimed in. "Do you know what it's called?"

"Oh. No," Tilly said. "Clara didn't say. I'll tell you tomorrow when we're back and you can see."

"Just stay safe, sweetheart," Grandma said. "Don't do anything rash. By the way, where did you pop my fairy-tale book once you'd finished with it? I can't find it."

"Oh," Tilly said, trying to think of what to say. "It's, uh, I think I put it on Grandad's desk?"

"Ah, okay," Grandma said. She didn't sound suspicious, as Tilly had never given them reason to be before, and Tilly immediately felt guilty and tried to change the subject.

"So, anything to report from the Underlibrary?" she asked.

"Really, you don't need to think about all of that," Grandad said. "Let us deal with it. We don't even need to talk about it, honestly." Then there was a pause, and Tilly could almost hear them nudging Bea to say something.

"Look after yourself, darling," Bea said vaguely.

"Just be safe, Tilly, sweetheart," Grandad said. "We love you so much."

"I promise," Tilly said. But she found that underneath the chilly feeling of guilt for lying to her grandparents about where the fairy-tale book was, there was something else stirring inside her: something rebellious and fiery and hard to ignore.

The next morning was a perfect winter day, skies so blue they looked as though you could sail in them. There was a just-the-right-side-of-sharp bite in the air, and softly falling snow made everything look as though it were dusted with icing sugar. Tilly found herself wishing Anne were there to enjoy it.

Clara was already up and dressed immaculately in lavender slim-cut pants with a black turtleneck and black boots. She was drinking espresso and reading a newspaper when Tilly came down for a breakfast of toasted brioche and hot chocolate. Oskar was buzzing with excitement over their bookshop visit.

After bundling up in coats and hats and scarves, they followed Clara back down the stairs and onto the street, where a black car waited. A smartly dressed man emerged and opened the passenger door for Clara, while Tilly and Oskar clambered into the back seat. The drive through the Parisian streets was short but there were so many things to take in—stylishly wrapped-up couples walking hand in hand, chocolate-box patisseries with windows piled high with impossibly beautiful cakes, and a drive over the Seine River that made Tilly feel as though she were in a film. After only five minutes they pulled up in a quiet, tiny, narrow street with no bookshop to be seen.

"This way," Clara said, heading to an unremarkable door.

On the stone wall there was a bell, and a discreet plaque with a gold circle around an intricate drawing of a feather. Above the illustration was written *The Faery Cabinet*. Clara pushed the door open and Tilly and Oskar followed, half expecting to be transported into a magical world.

The room was small, with a desk stacked high with books and a till wedged in among them. Halls and nooks and steps led off in several directions. As well as many, many bookshelves, the walls were covered with photos of smiling people, postcards, and notes. A ladder that had seen better days was leaning against one wall, and Tilly could see a much larger room through an archway straight ahead of them. Handwritten signs were pinned to several of the shelves to mark different genres, and jazz music played quietly. Behind the desk was a threadbare armchair, and in it was a woman with short gray hair and large tortoiseshell glasses, absorbed in a book. Clara gave a polite cough and the woman looked up.

"Clara! *On est gâté!*" she said, standing up, knocking over several books that had been balanced on the arm of her chair in the process. "*Et qui est-ce?*" she said, smiling at Tilly and Oskar, who looked at her in bemusement.

"Not French, I see," she said in English, with, to Tilly's surprise, an English accent. "Your grandson, by any chance?"

"He is indeed," Clara said, pushing Oskar forward to shake her hand.

"A pleasure, Oskar," the woman said. "My name is Gretchen.

It's wonderful to meet you after so long. And who's this?"

"This is my friend," Oskar explained. "She's staying with us for a few days before Christmas."

"Hello," Tilly said. "Your bookshop is very . . . full."

Gretchen laughed loudly and without self-consciousness. "You're not wrong," she said. "Now, Oskar neglected to mention your name. What shall I call you?"

"I'm Matilda," she said. "Matilda Pages. But everyone calls me Tilly."

"Matilda Pages," Gretchen said, looking intently at her. "Well, it is lovely to meet you. My name is Gretchen Stein. Welcome to the Faery Cabinet."

"And, Gretchen," Clara said, "just to add a *soupçon* of excitement to today, I believe my grandson and his friend are bookwanderers."

"*What?*" Oskar spluttered, spinning to face his grandmother. "How do you even know what that is?"

"Where do you think you got it from, *mon cher?*" Clara said, with a mischievous smile.

12

Find Your Own Path

O
skar was staring at Clara, dumbfounded.

"Sorry, what? You're a bookwanderer?"

"Why, yes," she said.

"Is Dad?"

"Sadly, I do not believe so," she said. "If one could artwander into a painting, I have no doubt he would be adept at that, and who knows, perhaps there is a secret community of these people we do not know about. But books, no."

"When did you realize I could bookwander too?"

"I did not know for certain," Clara said, smiling. "But, Matilda, I know of your grandparents, and so as soon as I heard your name, I thought it interesting that my grandson had become friends with you. And when you were asking to go to a bookshop, my heart sang a little as I thought perhaps it was true. And I am so happy to find myself correct!"

"So you're a bookwanderer too?" Tilly asked Gretchen.

"I am indeed," she said.

"Do you know my grandparents?"

"I know of them, yes," Gretchen said. "But I prefer to keep myself to myself. I was never one for all the rules and regulations of the Underlibraries. . . . I'm more of a free spirit. Speaking of which, you guys should go and have some fun! Find a book you'd like to visit!"

"I can't remember the last person who told us to have fun bookwandering," Tilly said, that rebellious feeling bubbling up inside her again. Maybe Oskar was right and she had been over-cautious, she thought. Gretchen and Clara were adults—and bookwanderers—and they clearly trusted her and Oskar. Her grandparents were just anxious because of what had happened to her mum, and that made sense, but they weren't here, and what they didn't know couldn't hurt them, right? She took a deep breath. "Shall we come and tell you when we've decided where to wander?"

"Whyever would you need to do that?" Gretchen replied.

"Well, in case something goes wrong, I suppose," Tilly said. "My grandparents like to know where we go, just in case. There are bad people out there—even bookwanderers."

"I mean, of course that's true," Gretchen said. "But there are bad people everywhere, even in the Underlibraries. Do you know—"

"Come now, Gretchen," Clara interrupted, laughing affectionately. "Just because you did not find a home at an

Underlibrary does not mean they aren't right for Tilly and Oskar. Now is not the time for conspiracy theories. We shall let Oskar and Matilda choose their own path, yes?"

"That's exactly my point!" Gretchen said. "Find your own path! Don't just blindly follow the one laid out in front of you."

"But I thought we had to follow Underlibrary rules?" Oskar said, and Gretchen rolled her eyes.

"Of course you don't," she said. "This bookshop doesn't. It's not on any Underlibrary map, or subject to any of their rules. I only recognize the authority of the Archivists—who don't meddle in individual people's lives."

"They do not meddle at all at the moment," Clara said. "Whether we want them to or not."

"But I thought the Archivists were just legends?" Tilly said.

"I bet those squares at the Underlibrary told you that, didn't they?" Gretchen groused, and Clara laid a conciliatory hand on her arm.

"The Archivists haven't been involved in bookwandering for many, many years now," she said. "And so we should not be surprised that many bookwanderers have ceased to believe in them with no evidence. But I still have faith that they would help if our need were dire."

"How would they know, though?" Tilly asked, thinking of Melville Underwood. "Can you, like, email them or something?"

"I do not think they have email," Clara said, smiling. "They say that there is a map to find them, but I am not sure if that is a story too, or whether anyone would know where to find it anymore."

"Someone must know," Tilly said, frustrated. "Otherwise, what's the point of having a map? What's the point of even having the Archivists, if we can't find them?"

"I cannot answer your question, I am afraid," Clara said. "Now, you two do some exploring, *oui*? Where would you like to go?" She cast her eyes around, and picked up a nondescript paperback book from a nearby shelf. "Here?"

"But this is a book of fairy tales," Tilly protested.

"You said you would like to read some old stories?" Clara prompted.

"Yes, but I meant read in the traditional sense," Tilly said. "My grandma told me we weren't allowed to bookwander into fairy tales, that they're dangerous!"

"Well, this *grand-mère* thinks you two can hold your own." Clara smiled.

Tilly and Oskar exchanged a look.

"I mean, if Mamie says it's okay . . ." Oskar said.

"So they're not really dangerous?" Tilly pushed.

"They're a little wilder than stories rooted in the written word, sure," Gretchen said. "But that's what makes them beautiful and exciting! You'll be fine in there—just keep hold of the book, stick together, avoid obviously dangerous situations. Common sense goes a long way."

"You're sure?" Oskar said directly to Clara, clearly

desperately wanting to trust his grandmother. "We've been told pretty directly that weird stuff goes on in them."

"There is 'weird stuff' in many places, Oskar," she said. "That is what makes life interesting, I think. But it is for you to decide, of course." She held a hand out for the book, but Oskar kept hold of it.

"But aside from the usual weird stuff," Tilly said. "We heard that it was worse than usual at the moment?"

"What do you mean?" Gretchen asked, a little sharply. "Where did you hear that?"

"From the Underlibrary," Tilly said. "We were told that things were more unstable than they'd ever been before. Had you heard that?"

"I think that's rather exaggerated," Gretchen said. "I visited the golden goose the other day and everything was fine—positively domestic."

"Did you go and get a golden egg?" Oskar said, eyes lighting up.

"If only!" Gretchen smiled. "You can't bring things out of books—you know that."

"But we saw a hat that . . ." Oskar paused and started again. "We have definitely seen someone bring something out of a book."

"And my mum brought something home too," Tilly said, thinking of the bee-shaped necklace she wore all the time. The one that matched the one her father had given Bea while inside *A Little Princess*.

"Well, I'm not sure what your mum brought home, or how," Gretchen said, giving Tilly another appraising look. "Or where the hat came from that you don't want to tell me about. But the rules are that you can't bring something that is of that particular story out. Obviously you can bring out things like the clothes you go in wearing—imagine if everyone's glasses disappeared as soon as they came out of a book! So the items you've seen must not have originated in the story they've come out of. So, sadly, no golden eggs for me."

"So you went into this book?" Oskar asked, eager to move the conversation away from Melville. He held up the fairy-tale collection he'd been given.

"That very one," Gretchen said. "So you can trust me. It was only the other day. How much can have changed since then?"

Tilly and Oskar climbed a steep, rickety set of stairs that led into another warren of rooms full of books, including one that housed a piano and a cat.

"How are you feeling?" Tilly asked Oskar carefully.

"It's just, like . . . imagine a family member keeping that big a secret from you for your whole life!" Oskar said, shell-shocked. Tilly raised an eyebrow at him. "Right, of course," he said. "Been there, done that."

"It does explain a lot, though," Tilly said. "About how you could bookwander with me and all of that. You were a book-wanderer all along."

"That's cool," Oskar said. "I'm not just the best-friend character anymore. I'm, like, legit magic in my own right."

"You were always magic in your own right," Tilly insisted, and Oskar grinned sheepishly, before sitting down at the piano and bashing out a very wonky version of "Chopsticks."

As he played, Tilly wandered the shelves, pulling books out at random and flicking through the pages until she noticed there was a pattern.

"Do you know," she said, starting to look properly, "a lot of these books are collections of fairy tales?" She opened the book she was holding at random and it was "Little Red Riding Hood." Again. *Weird*, she thought. *The same story I was reading on the train.*

"I guess she collects them?" Oskar said. "The shop is called the Faery Cabinet after all. And it's not like fairy tales are particularly unusual. How dangerous do you think they really are?" He held up the book Clara had given them downstairs.

"It's not that I don't trust Clara or Gretchen," Tilly said uneasily. "But Chalk is hiding in a fairy tale somewhere, and Underwood got lost in one for decades, and his sister got killed."

"We don't know that really happened," Oskar said. "I don't believe anything Melville says."

"Fair," Tilly said. "But I trust Grandma and Grandad and they seem pretty sure. Grandma's worked inside fairy tales, so she knows what she's talking about when it comes to bookwandering there."

"Yeah," Oskar agreed. "But I just think if Mamie says it's okay and we're doing it from here, then it's pretty low risk, right? And I just found out that I'm a full-on, in-my-blood bookwanderer! I want to do some bookwandering! And we can come straight back out again, I promise. Let's just go to a really boring one, just to see. How about 'Red Riding Hood'?" he suggested.

"I mean, safe apart from the wolf trying to eat everyone," Tilly said.

"But we'll just avoid that part!" Oskar said. "We'll go in at the very beginning—just to see!"

Tilly shrugged nervously. "Okay, then, but right at the beginning," she said, steeling herself. She thought about what Anne would do, and instantly felt a little braver.

Once upon a time there lived in a certain village a little country girl, the prettiest creature that was ever seen. Her mother was excessively fond of her; and her grandmother doted on her still more. This good woman had made for her a little red riding-hood; which became the girl so extremely well that everybody called her Little Red Riding-Hood.

The bookshop click-clacked around them, as though a plug had been pulled in the room, and the fabric of real life was sucked down under their feet.

Tilly and Oskar found themselves standing on the very edge of a wood, next to a pretty thatched cottage. The door opened as they arrived and out came a little girl holding a basket and wearing a bright red cloak.

Tilly and Oskar watched as she skipped away from the cottage and toward the woods.

"Looks normal to me!" Tilly said, trying not to think about the little girl wandering off into the dangerous forest. "Had enough?"

"The thing is," Oskar said, "I know we said we were going to avoid any mention of wolves, but I feel kind of weird about letting her just disappear off and get eaten."

"Isn't there a woodcutter around to help her?" Tilly said, trying to convince herself as much as Oskar.

"Not in this version," he replied, showing her the page he'd just checked. "She fully gets eaten."

"Well, she's not really real anyway, is she?" Tilly said quietly, watching the small girl walk into the shadowy trees. The problem was, though, she realized, as a cold feeling took root in her stomach, that if Red Riding Hood wasn't really real, then neither was her father, and then where did that leave her? If this wasn't real in some way, then neither was she. Tilly sighed, resigned. "I'm not helping if you get eaten by a wolf, though," she said to Oskar as they set off toward the woods.

13

What Great Teeth You Have

"Okay, so we'll just maybe try to get her to turn back, or not listen to the wolf?" Tilly said as they followed the girl into the woods.

"Great," Oskar said, stumbling over tree roots as he tried to read the story all the way through. "Okay, so it just says, 'as she was going through the wood' she met the wolf. Can you see anything?"

"No, still just her," Tilly said, peering into the trees.

"Okay, and then the wolf is too scared to eat her because there are woodcutters nearby, so he runs ahead, eats the grandmother, then waits for Red Riding Hood. Then he eats her."

"I guess these are the darker fairy tales that Clara was talking about," Tilly said. "I can see why they changed it in other versions."

"I guess we should warn her," Oskar said. "Should we catch up and talk to her, maybe?"

"This is your idea!" Tilly said. "Your idea—your plan."

"Fine, let's catch up, then," Oskar said, but before they could reach her, a lanky wolf loped out of the trees onto the path, stopping the girl in her tracks. Oskar pulled Tilly off the path and behind a tree, but Little Red Riding Hood didn't seem scared in the slightest and greeted the wolf with a curtsy as he circled her on the path.

"Whither are you going?" he drawled.

"I am going to see my grandmamma," Red Riding Hood replied politely. "To carry her a cake and a little pot of butter from my mamma."

"Does she live far off?" the wolf asked, licking his lips hungrily.

"Oh! Aye," the little girl said. "It is beyond that mill you see there, at the first house in the village."

"Well, I shall go and see her too. I'll go this way, and you go that, and we shall see who will be there soonest." And at that the wolf ran back into the trees and disappeared from sight within seconds.

"Okay, I don't want to seem rude, but is she completely daft?" Oskar whispered to Tilly. "Does she not know he wants to eat her?"

"Apparently not," Tilly said. "But quick, we need to tell her so we can all get to her grandmother's house before the wolf." They headed back onto the path and quickly caught up with Red Riding Hood, who was ambling along singing to herself, picking flowers and getting distracted by passing butterflies.

"Excuse me," Tilly said, tapping her on the shoulder. The girl turned around but, just as when she had encountered a talking wolf, didn't seem especially concerned or surprised.

"Why, hello, would you like to know where I am going?"

"You should probably stop volunteering that information," Oskar said. "Just a tip."

"I am going to visit my grandmother! She lives by the mill, which you can see just there, and it's the first house you come to after that," she went on.

"May we come with you?" Tilly asked.

"Why, of course, and it is such a beautiful day to be out in the woods."

"Don't you think we should go a little faster?" Oskar suggested. "You did just tell a wolf where to find your grandmother."

"Yes, he said we would see who would get there the quickest! What larks!"

"I think his plan is to make sure he is the fastest," Tilly said, trying to stay calm. "I don't want to upset you, but I'm not sure that the wolf is going to simply say hello to your grandmother. I think she might be in danger."

"From the wolf?" Red Riding Hood said, astonished. "Whyever would you think that?"

"Well, he's a wolf, and wolves eat people. . . ."

"You think he means to eat my grandmother?" She gasped, putting a dainty hand to her mouth in shock.

"YES!" Oskar said, impatient. "That's what wolves do!"

"Goodness," Red Riding Hood said, chucking her bunch of flowers over her shoulder. "I suppose we should get going, then. This path is actually a direct way to the village, but let us hope Mr. Wolf encounters something to slow him down on his way!"

"Finally," Tilly said under her breath. "By the way, what's your real name?"

Red Riding Hood looked blankly at her.

"Why, everyone just knows me as Red Riding Hood, because of my red cloak." She stopped and twirled around as she said it. Tilly and Oskar stared at each other in disbelief.

"It's a lovely cloak," Tilly said, "but we need to keep moving."

"And we meant, like, what is your real name?" Oskar pushed on. "What did your parents call you before you had your red cloak?"

"Do you know, I'm not sure I've ever been known any other way?" she said, confusion momentarily flitting across her face. "I suppose I must have had another name at some point, but I can't think of it at all. How strange." She shrugged, and the bewilderment vanished. "Oh well! You can call me Red, for short, if you wish."

Tilly doubted whether they had any chance of beating the wolf to Red's grandmother's cottage, but as they turned a corner the trees started to thin out and the mill itself came into view, a cottage tucked just behind it.

"There it is!" Red said. "Oh, and there's Mr. Wolf!" The wolf was prowling around the cottage walls.

"Oskar, quick!" Tilly hissed. "Distract him before he knocks on the door!"

"*What?*" Oskar said, horrified. "How am I supposed to do that?"

"If only we could somehow get inside and warn her," Red said, still seeming to lack any particular urgency or fear.

"That's a brilliant idea," Tilly said, suddenly realizing that was exactly what they could do. She found the line in the story where the wolf knocks on the door, and grabbed Oskar and Red by the hand. "Let's fast-forward a little bit. . . ."

Suddenly they were inside the cottage, hearing the knocking outside. A frail-looking woman was lying in a bed, staring at them, and a warm fire burned in the grate. Tilly was about to try to explain why they had just magically appeared inside her home when the woman spoke.

"Red! How kind of you to come and visit your ill grandmamma!"

"Why is no one surprised by any of the seriously strange stuff that's going on?" Oskar whispered to Tilly.

"My dears, will one of you kindly open the door? I think someone else is here. Perhaps it is that handsome woodcutter who has been visiting me every once in a while."

"Maybe we should ask who it is before we open the door?" Tilly suggested hurriedly. "Who's there?" she called.

"Your grandchild, Little Red Riding Hood," came a bizarre high-pitched squeak, which sounded nothing at all like Red, "who has brought you a cake, and a little pot of butter."

"How curious," Grandmamma said. "For you are in here! I wonder who it could be? Red, won't you go and see?"

"Goodness me, these people," Tilly said, standing in between Red and the door. "It's the wolf out there! He wants to come in and eat us all! We mustn't open the door!"

Oskar came and joined her and they peered out of the window from underneath a corner of the lacy curtains. The wolf paced in front of the door, looking over his shoulder, presumably for Red.

"Do you think he'll give up and go away?" Oskar asked hopefully.

"I doubt it," Tilly said. "He looks pretty hungry. And eating these two is basically his whole motivation, so I'm not sure what else he'd do. I'm trying to think of what happens in the other versions of the story."

"This version does mention woodcutters existing, so could we sneak out and try to find one?"

"Maybe, although—"

Their whispered planning was abruptly interrupted by a swish and a thwack and a howl. Oskar and Tilly looked out of the window to see a girl wielding an ax and standing over what looked to be a rather dead wolf. This girl didn't look much older than them but was wearing black woolen pants tucked into knee-high leather boots, with a sturdy tunic over the top. As well as the ax she was holding, she had a sword tucked into her belt. Her black hair was woven into tight braids, keeping it away from her face, and around her shoulders was a burgundy red cloak.

"If she wasn't in here with us . . ." Oskar said.

". . . you would say she looked like Red Riding Hood," Tilly said, and they turned to look at the girl in the cottage, who had gone to sit on her grandmother's bed.

"Grandmamma, what great arms you have got!" she was saying.

"All the better to hug thee, my dear," Grandmamma said, gathering Red into an affectionate embrace.

"And what great ears you have got!"

"That is to hear the better, my child."

Tilly and Oskar looked at each other in disbelief.

"She has totally normal-sized ears," Tilly called over. "And actually quite frail-looking arms."

She went over to the bed and waved her hand in between Red and Grandmamma.

"Well, guys," she said. "It's been . . . an experience meeting you both, but the wolf situation seems to have been dealt with, so we're going to head home."

"Good-bye now, dears!" Grandmamma said, and Red didn't even seem to notice them leaving.

"What great teeth you have!" she said merrily to her grandmother, who chortled along with her.

Tilly and Oskar pushed open the door cautiously, aware there was a girl with an ax on the other side.

"Hello," she said cheerfully, wiping wolf blood from the ax blade.

"Hello," Tilly started. "Who are you, if you don't mind me asking?"

"I'm Red," she said, holding out the non-ax-holding hand to shake. "I see you had a wolf problem."

14

Prince Charming, at Your Service

Tilly looked at the dead wolf on the ground, feeling a little nauseous.

"Thank you," she said nervously. "But . . ."

"But there's someone else who calls herself Red inside that house," Oskar took over. "Is that where you live too?"

"Ugh, no," the other Red said, rolling her eyes. "I cannot stand that girl. Empty-headed child. Always getting herself into trouble—no sense of self-preservation at all."

"But you can't both be Little Red Riding Hood!" Oskar said.

"Excuse me, I'll ask you not to call me that," this Red said, staring daggers at Oskar. "A childhood nickname I'd rather leave behind."

"Yep, of course, sorry," Oskar said, eyeing the ax. "My mistake."

"Anyway, if you two can take it from here, I'll be on my way," Red said. "There's a local woodcutter I'm teaching some ax skills to—don't want to be late." And with that she pulled her hood up over her hair and stalked away into the forest.

"That was very strange," Oskar said, watching her go.

"It's what Grandma and Grandad were talking about, though, isn't it?" Tilly said. "Fairy tales going wonky, characters being in the wrong place. We need to get back to the Faery Cabinet before anything weirder happens. We should be glad we haven't stumbled across anything worse."

"Agreed," Oskar said, opening the book up and beginning to read. Moments later they found themselves standing off to one side of a very sorry-looking cottage with weather-beaten walls and several holes in its thatched roof.

"Okay, well, this isn't the bookshop," Tilly said. "What did you do?"

"I just read the last line of the story," Oskar said, showing Tilly the page.

"Oh, but that's just the last line of Red Riding Hood's story," she said, pointing. "So I guess we're now at the start of the next story, which is . . ." She turned the page to look for the title but Oskar was already speaking.

"'Jack and the Beanstalk'!" he said.

"Yes! How did you know?" Tilly asked, looking up to see him pointing beyond the cottage. Behind it was one of the most bizarre things Tilly had ever seen, even in Wonderland. A huge green plant had sprung up so quickly that it had ruptured the ground around it. Cracks and huge furrows stretched out for meters and meters from the base, uprooting other trees and plants, and knocking over hedges and fences. The beanstalk was as thick as a London bus standing on one end, and was an unnaturally bright green, as though it had been colored in with wax crayons by a child. Even stranger than all of that was how it looked as though it had grown in a way that made it designed to be climbed. A rough pattern spiraled around the stalk like a staircase, and branches grew out of it at regular intervals, forming themselves into a makeshift set of railings and handholds. For a few moments, Tilly and Oskar simply stood and stared up at it, but their concentration was abruptly broken by a cacophony of curses and shouts of pain. Suddenly a boy slid down the final few meters of stalk-steps, bounced through the lower branches, and landed at the bottom of the beanstalk in an ungraceful heap.

"Should we go and help him?" Oskar whispered. "That must be Jack, right?"

"I guess so," Tilly said. "He's a goody, isn't he, so it can't do any harm." They walked toward him and heard a squawk emanate from under him, just as he noticed them approaching. He waved merrily, and rolled over to reveal a disgruntled-looking hen, half-squashed underneath him.

"It's really hard to climb down a giant beanstalk while carrying a hen," he said, picking a stray feather off his pants. "She seems all right, though." The hen regarded him and let out an unimpressed cluck. "I'm Jack," he said, sticking out a slightly dirty-looking hand.

"Tilly," Tilly said, shaking it.

"I'm Oskar," Oskar said. "And you're Jack. Jack and the Beanstalk."

"Well, my name is Jack, and I did grow this beanstalk—albeit accidentally—so yes, I suppose so," Jack said. "It's quite catchy that, isn't it? Jack and the Beanstalk." He swooped an open palm through the sky as if imagining his name in lights.

"Are you guys hungry?" Jack asked. "Do you want to come in for . . . Well, I'm not sure what we've got, it might just be water, but you're very welcome to share. I need to tell my mother what I've found—it's going to make us a fortune!" He held up the bedraggled hen. "Her eggs are going to make me rich!"

"Are eggs . . . especially expensive here?" Oskar said, confused.

"Her eggs will be," Jack said smugly, and Tilly finally figured it out.

"Oh, of course," she said. "You stole the hen from the giant at the top of the beanstalk."

"Hey, how do you know about that?" Jack said, looking nervously up the beanstalk, which disappeared into the clouds.

"Just a hunch," Tilly tried to cover. "I'd heard there were giants around here who had, you know, magical stuff."

Jack gave her an appraising look. "Well, don't tell anyone," he said. "Otherwise everyone will be trying to get their hands on a hen like this. Anyway, are you coming? My mam's face is going to be a picture when she hears!"

Tilly and Oskar exchanged a look.

"It can't do any harm now we're here!" Oskar whispered. "And I'm starving. We'll just have a quick snack and then head back."

"Fine," Tilly said, and they followed Jack toward the cottage.

The door of the cottage looked like it had been blue at some point, but the paint had nearly all peeled off, and the whole door was hanging from one hinge.

"It's not much but it's home," Jack said, pushing the door open. They followed him into a very dim, dank room with an empty fireplace against one wall. There was barely any furniture, but sitting at a rough wooden table was a woman who looked impatiently at Jack.

"Where have you been?" she demanded. "And who are these children you've brought back with you? You know we don't have anything to feed them with. I hope you're not here begging!" she said, narrowing her eyes at Tilly and Oskar. "And we've not got nothing to steal if that's what you're thinking!"

"They're friends, Mam," Jack said. "And wait until you see what I've brought home—it's going to turn our fortunes right around."

His mother did not look convinced. "I've not much faith in your schemes, son," she said, before turning to the others. "You see that monstrosity sitting out there in our back garden?"

"It's quite hard to miss," Tilly said.

"Exactly," his mother said. "And do you know where this beanstalk came from? I'll tell you," she went on, not pausing to let them answer. "Yesterday, after eating the last few scraps of stale bread for our breakfast, I realized the time had finally come. If we had any hope of making it through another winter, the only thing to do was to send Jack off to market with our cow. Our only cow. You might even say our beloved cow."

"Oh, come off it, Mam," Jack said. "You hated the sight of her."

"She may have been a grumpy old thing but she gave us milk, didn't she?" she said. "And I wouldn't have parted with her if we hadn't been so desperate. Anyway, this one," she continued, nodding at Jack, "takes her down to the market, bright and early, and I say to him, make sure you get a good price. Don't let no one take advantage of you and your soft-heartedness. So off he went, and before he'd even had time to get to the market, he was back here—no cow in sight. But do you know what he did have? Not coins. Oh no. He had beans. Beans! The boy had traded our last chance of a livelihood and sustenance for a handful of beans."

"They were magic beans!" Jack said. "And you didn't believe me. And look."

"I tell you, who wants the sort of magic that grows giant inedible plants in your garden?" his mother said. "I'll admit I didn't believe there was any magic in them beans at all. I was all set to boil them up for dinner, before I realized they weren't even any good for eating. So I chucked them out of that there window, and now look. A magic plant." She rolled her eyes. "How about a magic money tree or some magic never-ending bread or a magic cow, how about that?"

"How about a magic hen?" Jack asked, a mischievous twinkle in his eye.

"Aye, I'm sure," his mother said. "And what would she do—lay magic eggs?"

As if on cue the hen let out an almighty squawk, and stood up on spindly legs to reveal a golden egg.

"How did you do that?" Jack's mother said. "Is it a trick?"

"No!" Jack said. "I went to see what was up at the top of the beanstalk. . . ."

"You did what?" she shrieked. "What would I have done if you'd fallen and broken your neck!"

"Well, I did go up there, and I found her," Jack finished calmly.

"You found her up there?" she said. "What, just wandering around in the clouds?"

"Basically, yes," Jack said.

"And she was just wandering around up there on her own, you're trying to tell me? Just you, the sky, and this one hen?" his mother pushed on.

"There was only one hen if that's what you're asking," Jack said.

"She didn't belong to no one? I don't want no angry farmers

chasing me down trying to claim back their magic hen now."

"Not a farmer exactly," Jack said, choosing his words carefully. His mother tapped her foot and waited for him to tell her the whole truth. "More like a . . . giant."

"A giant!" his mother shrieked. "You stole a magic hen from a giant? What possessed you, Jack? I tell you, it'll be you answering the door when he comes knocking!"

"He won't," Jack said, sounding a little uncertain. "I don't think he even saw me."

"He doesn't think!" she repeated sarcastically. "He can't be sure but he doesn't think the giant saw him steal his property! Let's hope he's a vegetarian giant!"

"Actually, he was quite specific about eating meat," Jack said. "Had a whole song about it, in fact."

"Oh, we've got ourselves a carnivorous, musically talented giant, have we? That makes it all better."

"Calm down, Mam," Jack said. "He doesn't know who I am."

"No, of course not, the plant leading right down into our back garden won't give us away for sure," she said. "Let's hope all his talents lie in music, and none in his sense of direction! And what have I told you about telling me to calm down!"

Tilly had started flicking through the fairy-tale book to get her and Oskar out of there, but the rustling pages caught Jack's mother's attention and she advanced on them wielding a broom in one hand.

"You two in your funny clothes," she said. "Did you put him up to this whole hen-stealing lark?"

"No!" Oskar said. "We weren't even there, I promise!"

She regarded them with deep suspicion.

"He may be a soft-hearted lad, but he's not stupid. Stealing from a giant, now, I don't believe he'd do that of his own accord." She looked as though she were about to give someone a thwap with her broom when there was a sound like all the air being sucked out of the room. Tilly and Oskar held their hands to their heads as their ears popped, as though they were on a plane taking off. Once they recovered they realized, in alarm, that something very odd had happened to Jack and his mother. They looked like characters in a glitching video game, hovering and flickering as if they were barely present, although when Oskar went over to poke Jack, he could still feel the rough wool of his clothes.

"You've never seen this happen before, right?" Oskar said, sounding nervous.

"No," Tilly said.

And then, all of a sudden, Jack went completely still before shattering into millions of tiny pieces, like a glass vase that had been dropped on the floor.

Tilly's face went white as she stepped over to look at where Jack had been standing.

"That wasn't there before, was it?" she said, gingerly poking at a sticky black puddle on the floor with the toe of her boot.

"What is it?" Oskar said, coming over. "Melted book character?"

"It looks like ink," Tilly said.

"You're right," Oskar said.

Tilly got down on her knees to look more closely. Just as she stuck a finger out to touch it, though, the black liquid abruptly vanished, as though it had been instantaneously absorbed by the stone floor. At that same moment, the cottage door banged open and they all looked up to see Jack walking in smiling, a hen under his arm. As he entered the cottage, his mother came back into focus, broom still in hand, and mid-sentence, angrily shouting at the spot where Tilly and Oskar had been standing.

"So, if you two . . ." She stopped, realizing she was talking to the air. She spun around, confused.

"Mam!" Jack said. "You'll never guess what I have!"

"What are you doing here?" she said, suspiciously staring at Tilly and Oskar.

"Oh, hello," Jack said to them. "Are you friends of my mother's?"

"No, they're rascals who wandered in off the road while I had my back turned, trying to keep this place clean and tidy," she said, coming for them with the broom. "Out! Out! Before I report you!" Tilly and Oskar let themselves be swept from the room, relieved to get out of the cottage, but Jack followed them.

"I'm sorry," he said. "Mam can be a bit . . . protective."

"That's one word for it," Oskar said under his breath.

"Well, we should be going now," Tilly said politely. "Sorry to bother you!"

"Now hang on," Jack said. "Don't be dashing off so quickly; we only just met! What are your names? Are you from the village? I don't recognize you at all."

"Haven't we already done this?" Oskar said.

"Done what?" Jack asked.

"Nothing. He's just a bit, er, jet-lagged, I think," Tilly covered. "I'm Tilly—and he's Oskar."

"Jet-lagged?" Jack repeated.

"We've just been traveling for a while," Oskar said, trying to get back on track. "And we really do need to be getting home."

"Where's home for you?" Jack said, incorrigibly friendly. "I can walk with you?"

"We're fine by ourselves, honestly," Tilly said. She went to take a step backward, and felt the gravel of the road crunch under her shoes. "Although it's very nice of you to offer."

"Hang on," Jack said, coming closer.

"No, honestly, we're fine!" she said, walking backward into the middle of the road.

"No, I just meant—" he said, but at that moment there was a whoosh of hooves and a horse flew around the corner, causing Tilly to jump to one side, falling to the ground as she did so. ". . . that you need to be careful of riders," Jack finished weakly, before rushing over to make sure she was okay.

"I'm fine," she said breathlessly, shocked but unhurt except for a grazed knee and a rip in her tights. "It didn't hit me."

The rider was pulling to a stop and backing the horse around.

"Hey there, miss, what are you doing in my way?" the rider asked. He was absurdly handsome, with a perfectly straight nose and chocolatey-brown eyes. He wore layers of obviously expensive velvet clothes, and his hat was topped with an extravagantly large collection of feathers.

"I'm sorry," Tilly said, automatically apologizing. "I didn't see you coming."

"You should look where you're going," Oskar said. "It's not your way!"

"Why, yes," the man said. "All the roads in this kingdom belong to my father, the King, and will belong to me when I marry and inherit the crown."

"Okay, I can see how from that perspective this is literally your way," Oskar muttered. "But you should still look where you are going."

"But, young sir, I have more important things to think about—namely, love, the greatest quest of them all. I am in search of a fabled princess whose hand I intend to win through my bravery and charm." He doffed his hat in an elaborate twirl. "Prince Charming, at your service. But not really at your service, you understand, it's a symbolic thing. I'm a prince—I'm not going to actually help you with anything."

"Right, then," Oskar said. "Good luck with that."

"I seek the tower where the princess is imprisoned by a malevolent witch," he said. "Have any of you heard tell of this mysterious and evil place where my love and her lustrous hair are confined?"

"Oh, you're looking for Rapunzel," Oskar said. The prince made his horse trot closer to Oskar, and peered down at him.

"You know of her, boy?" he asked.

"I haven't met her," Oskar said slowly. "But I've . . . well, I've heard of her."

"You mean to say news of her beauty and kindness and

peril have traveled far and wide?" the prince said in alarm.

"I think the news has gotten out, yes," Oskar said, unable to resist teasing the oblivious prince. "I actually think I read something about her."

"You have read proclamations of her ordeal!" the prince said. "I must away; there is no time to lose! I cannot risk another prince stealing her affections before I have a chance to prove myself and rescue her! You!" He pointed at Oskar. "You seem to know of her story; you shall come with me."

"Oh, no, thanks," Oskar said firmly. "I don't really know anything useful—such as where she is. I also don't want to help you."

"And we really need to get home," Tilly said, taking a step back toward Jack.

"Young squire, you misunderstand me," Prince Charming said, reaching down and grabbing Oskar by the scruff of his neck, swinging him up onto his horse in front of him. "You are my subject and I need your aid. You will attend me."

"Now hang on," Oskar said, trying to slide back down the horse, but Charming kept a strong arm wrapped around him and kicked his horse into a gallop. And before Tilly had quite realized what was going on, they had left in a cloud of dust.

15

The Three Bears

Tilly tried to get her breathing under control as she watched Oskar disappear off down the road. Jack, however, didn't seem especially perturbed.

"Good luck to him, I say!" he said, waving after them. "He seemed quite friendly, I thought. I've never met a prince before!"

"Firstly, he was awful," Tilly said. "But way more important, Jack, I really need to get Oskar back. I can't go home without him. And didn't you notice that Oskar really didn't want to help?"

"Oh," Jack said, deflated. "Well, do you want me to help find him?"

"Yes, please," Tilly said. "As quickly as possible! Do you know where Rapunzel's tower is?"

"I'm afraid not," Jack said. "But I do know someone who might. . . . Let's stop in with the Three Bears."

Tilly and Jack set off down the road, past a wooden signpost with pointers toward "Forest," "Castle," and "Village." Before too long they ended up at a quaint thatched cottage with a beautifully manicured garden and three rocking chairs of different sizes on the porch. A picturesque twist of smoke curled out of the chimney and the smell of freshly baked bread wafted in their direction. Jack pushed open the white gate and Tilly followed him up a garden path lined with flowering lavender plants buzzing with honeybees.

"The Bears are lovely," Jack said. "But do just be aware that they can be a bit jumpy around visitors. There's this local girl who used to keep sneaking in while they were out, and messing with their stuff and eating their food, and now she just wanders in any time of day and acts like it's her house."

"She's blonde, right?" Tilly said, knowing exactly who he was talking about.

"I don't know; I've never met her—have you?" Jack said, confused. "I thought you weren't from around here. Anyway, just don't touch anything without asking and you'll be fine." He knocked on the cotton-candy-pink door, and it opened to reveal a very large brown bear wearing a flowered apron and pink cat-eye glasses.

"Jack, my darling!" she said in a high-pitched growly sort of voice, kissing him on both cheeks. "And you've brought a visitor. How . . . delightful." She eyed Tilly up and down suspiciously. Tilly followed Jack over a welcome mat into a pristine kitchen connected to a beautiful living room. Everything was decorated in shades of rose pink and white, with gold accents, and the whole house smelled of fresh bread and clean linen. The bear put out her paw and shook hands gracefully with Tilly.

"Welcome to our home," she said. "Please take your shoes off and make yourself comfortable. But don't even think about eating anything. Sorry, I'm getting carried away!" She giggled nervously. "My name is Mummy Bear. Let me put the kettle on!" She retreated to the stove and put a pink kettle on to boil. "Now, Jack, my love, have you been into the village recently? Did you hear that the old lady at the end of the street—you know, the one who lives in a shoe—has taken up with the woodcutter? They were seen dining together only last night! Can you imagine! But enough about them; you know I can't abide gossip. How are you?"

"Oh, you know," Jack said, stretching his arms out. "I traded Mam's cow for some magic beans, accidentally grew a huge beanstalk, stole a magical hen from a giant. Bit of this, bit of that."

"Oh, Jack, you are a sort," Mummy Bear said affectionately. "Now, did I tell you that I heard there's some kind of competition going on at the castle because the King can't work out where his twelve daughters are going every night? He's offering any one of them for marriage if someone can solve the mystery! Can you imagine!"

"Do the daughters get a say?" Tilly couldn't help but ask, even though she knew the story of the Twelve Dancing Princesses and was well aware they didn't.

"Whyever would you think that?" Mummy Bear smiled at Tilly. "What a thought! Letting a princess choose her own husband! Whatever next!"

"What's that I heard about husbands?" a deep voice boomed, and down the stairs came an even bigger bear, wearing a tie complete with a tiepin clipping it to his fur, and a big gold watch on his huge, hairy wrist. He gave Jack a slap on the back that nearly winded him, and gave Mummy Bear a kiss on the nose that made her giggle.

"Guys," a squeaky voice said, and a very tiny bear emerged down the stairs wearing thick-rimmed glasses and a tutu. "Stop being so embarrassing."

"Sorry, Baby Bear," Daddy Bear said, giving Mummy Bear a tickle.

"Ughhh," Baby Bear said, ambling off again, with its paws over its ears.

"But I'm being a terrible host!" Daddy Bear said, walking over to Tilly, who involuntarily shrank back a little bit. He really was a very large bear.

"No need to be afraid, new friend!" he boomed. "Not unless you've got your fingers in our porridge! Only joking, only joking!"

"I'm Tilly," she said, nervously putting a hand out.

"And what brings you here today?" Daddy Bear asked, trying to shake her hand as gently as possible.

"Well, actually we were hoping you might be able to help us find someone," Tilly started. "They just passed this way."

"Did we see anyone, my dear?" Daddy Bear called to Mummy Bear.

"Oh, I wouldn't know!" she called. "What do you take me for, someone who watches from behind their curtains on the off chance that they see something scandalous? I would never!" She absentmindedly straightened the lacy curtains, which were a little askew.

"Well, I did," a twinkly voice said from the doorway, and everyone turned to see a radiantly beautiful young woman standing in the doorway, framed in sunlight. Jack was staring at her as if she were made of magic beans. The Bears looked less enthusiastic.

"Did you see a man on a horse, with a boy?" Tilly said eagerly.

"I'm not really sure," she said. "I wasn't paying attention, to be honest. I think it was a horse. Could have been a donkey. Or a rabbit. But who cares, really?"

"I do!" Tilly said. "It's actually quite important, if you wouldn't mind trying to—"

"Maybe it shall come back to me once I've rested and refreshed myself," the woman said, sitting down on the sofa, before grimacing and moving to a love seat, then frowning and settling in a cozy armchair. "Just right," she said, smiling.

"But could I just ask you exactly what you did see?" Tilly pressed on. "If you could try very hard to remember. There was a prince, and—"

"A prince!" Goldilocks shrieked. "Whyever didn't you say before that there was a prince? I would have paid way more attention if I'd known that!"

"He's actually already got his eyes set on Rapunzel," Jack said, unable to peel his own eyes from Goldilocks. "So I think he's, sort of, unavailable."

Goldilocks pouted.

"Rapunzel, you say?" Mummy Bear said.

"Yes!" Tilly said, desperately wanting to steer the conversation back on track. "Do you know where she lives?"

"Oh, have you heard the same rumors I have?" Mummy Bear said conspiratorially. "Of course I don't like to follow gossip, but I did hear word that she went through the crack in the sky. But it came via Tom Thumb, who heard it from Rumpelstiltskin, so who knows if it's true."

"Do you know where that is?" Tilly turned to Jack impatiently. "The crack in the sky?"

"Yes," he said slowly. "I do. But I've never been through before."

"It looks ever so dangerous," Mummy Bear said. "Do be careful."

"I promise," Jack said affectionately. "We'll just go and have a look and see if we can find any clues."

"Great!" Tilly said, springing to her feet. "Can we go now?" She heard a not-very-well-disguised tut of annoyance from Mummy Bear.

"I'm so sorry to dash off," Tilly said, trying to placate her. "It's just that we've lost my best friend, and his father will be so worried if we don't get him back before dinner! Thank you ever so much for having us—your house is very lovely!"

Tilly glared at Jack, who thankfully got the cue. He approached Goldilocks to say good-bye but she steadfastly ignored him, focusing instead on her immaculately painted fingernails.

"Come back anytime, Tilly," Mummy Bear said, not sounding especially sincere. "And do tell me what that Rapunzel is like, Jack. I've heard her hair is as beautiful as spun gold. Can you imagine?"

"Hmph," Goldilocks said. "I doubt it. More like straw, I've heard."

After a round of hugs from the Three Bears, Jack and Tilly were back on their way.

"So, what's the crack in the sky?" Tilly asked as they walked.

"It's just what it sounds like," he said. "It's not too far from here. Oh, shoot." He stopped walking. "I've left my golden egg at the Bears' cottage."

"Do you need it right now?" Tilly said, impatient to be on the way.

"Yes," Jack said. "It's my lucky charm! Not to mention it might be the only one she ever lays!"

"Okay, fine," Tilly said, turning around. "Let's be quick."

They half walked, half jogged back toward the Three Bears' cottage, and Jack knocked again, but there was no answer.

"How strange," Jack said. "It's been, what, five minutes since we left?" He knocked again, more firmly this time, and then tried to look through the windows. "I can't see anything," he said. "It's very dark in there—like all the lights are turned off." He looked worried, and came back to the door, shrugged, and turned the round gold handle, gently pushing the door open a crack.

"Anyone home?" he called. "It's Jack and Tilly! Oh—" He stopped talking abruptly and swung the door open so Tilly could see. It opened onto nothing. Just blackness,

with no light,

no shade,

no edges.

Nothing.

16

The Crack in the Sky

"What's . . . What is that?" Tilly whispered to Jack, feeling queasy. "Where are they?"

"I don't know," he said, the color draining from his face. "I hope they're okay. Do you think they're okay?" He was starting to sound panicked, and Tilly tried to calm him down, but she had no more idea of what was going on than he did, and no sensible suggestions. It didn't exactly look promising for the Three Bears, and everything that went wrong in this fairy-tale land seemed to make it less and less likely that she'd be able to find Oskar, let alone get them both home in one piece. Why hadn't she listened to her grandparents? It wasn't like she hadn't been told that fairy tales were dangerous. But just then Tilly remembered what Clara and Gretchen had said, and she stood a little more upright. If her grandparents didn't think she could cope here, then it was up to her to prove them wrong. She knew how bookwandering worked; she had the book from the Faery Cabinet and all she had to do was find Oskar.

"Right," she said firmly, as much to herself as to Jack. "We need a plan. I'm just going to have a look in my book. . . ."

"What is that going to tell you?" Jack said, pacing up and down.

"Books are always a good place to look for guidance," Tilly said. "Usually in a more metaphorical sense, but I think in this situation, we might be able to get a bit of practical advice. Here's hoping, anyway. . . ."

Tilly took a few steps back, away from Jack, and ran her finger down the list of story titles on the contents page.

"Okay, here," she said to herself. "'Goldilocks and the Three Bears,' page eighty-four; let's see what it says." She opened the book at page eighty-four, hoping there'd be a clue, but it was completely blank. There was the story title at the top of the page, but nothing else, and the next three pages were empty as well. Tilly started flicking through the book, and while most of the pages looked normal, there was another story missing. "Snow White and the Seven Dwarfs" was also blank. She turned to Jack.

"I don't suppose you know where a group of seven dwarfs live?" she asked. "They might have a woman living with them who's got skin as white as snow and lips as red as blood and hair as black as ebony?"

"You mean Snow White?" Jack

said. "You know her, too? It's so strange we've never met before—we have so many friends in common!"

"I only know her by reputation," Tilly said. "But I think she might know something about what's going on here. Can you take me to her?"

"I'm not allowed!" Jack said, working himself up again. "I promised! She's hiding from her wicked stepmother, who wants to kill her! Hardly anyone even knows she's staying with the Seven Dwarfs. Not even Mummy Bear! Have you told anyone else?"

"Not a soul," Tilly promised. "But I think if we want to find Oskar—and the Three Bears—we need to start there."

"You're sure?" Jack said.

"It's the best clue we've gotten so far," Tilly said resolutely. "So it's worth a shot."

They had only been walking for a few minutes when two small children burst out of the trees, holding hands. The little boy let out a squawk of terror when he saw Tilly, and the girl put her fists up, trying to disguise the fear on her face.

"I'm not going to hurt you!" Tilly said. "Are you okay? Are you lost?"

"Not anymore," the girl said, close to tears, and still half-heartedly holding her tiny fists up.

"We're going home," the boy said, pulling at the girl's hand. "Come on, Gretel."

"Are you going into the forest?" Gretel said to Tilly, wiping her nose with the back of her hand.

Jack nodded.

"You can have these, then," the girl said, looking at Tilly again and then pushing a small cloth bag into her hand, before letting the boy pull her toward the village.

"Gretel, as in Hansel and—" Tilly said.

"You know them, too!" Jack interrupted. "It's quite awkward actually, don't you think? The way their father keeps trying to get rid of them and they keep finding their way back. It's getting a bit embarrassing."

"But they're just tiny!" Tilly said in horror.

"Don't be fooled by their tears," Jack said. "They're pretty fierce. And they've got a sixth sense for home. And more tricks up their sleeves than they let on. I heard they pushed a witch into an oven! They always find their way home, although why they want to go back to their useless dad is another question."

Tilly opened the bag in her hand and saw a few bread crumbs left, as she had suspected she might. She slipped the bag into her pocket.

"Okay, I've got it," Jack said. He had been counting trees and bushes, trying to figure something out. "I think. I'm, like, eighty-percent sure I've got it. Tenth tree from the bramble bush, and then four toadstools to the left. Or was it four trees from the holly bush and then eight four-leaf clovers to the right? No, ten trees . . ." Jack kept repeating this to himself as he walked over to a tangled bramble bush covered in little yellow flowers. "Yes, this is it," he said much more confidently to Tilly. As he counted ten trees in from the outside of the forest, it started to get dark alarmingly quickly, and ominous owl hoots echoed through the branches. At the tenth tree, Jack looked down at his feet, seeing a cluster of red toadstools with white spots. From there, an unusually straight line of them headed off from the tree, and four toadstools later they found themselves at the base of a huge twisted oak tree. Its roots spilled out from the ground and wove under and over each other, and its huge trunk stretched up into the forest canopy.

"This is it!" Jack said, as if there hadn't been any doubt that he knew where he was going. He led Tilly around the trunk to a small red door almost entirely hidden among the tree roots. Jack crouched down and knocked on it three times.

"Hello?" he called. "Snow? Graham? Geoff? Is anyone home?" His optimism waned far faster than it had at the Three Bears' cottage, and with a grim look on his face, he pushed the door firmly. It swung open to reveal the same dark void that had been inside the Bears' cottage.

Tilly swallowed nervously and tried to summon her earlier determination. Jack picked up a stone from the ground and tossed it into the blackness, where it was immediately swallowed up. There was no sound of it hitting the inside of the tree or water or anything at all.

"This can't be good," Jack said. "I think we should catch up with the prince and your friend. Maybe we can ask Prince Charming if the King or Queen know anything about what's happening. And then I must get back to my mam, if she's still there."

"I'm sure everyone is okay," Tilly said, trying to comfort Jack, although she was not at all sure. "I think they've just gotten lost temporarily."

Jack nodded, and put on a brave smile. "Let's go, then," he said. "To the crack in the sky."

They closed the little red door carefully and walked back out of the forest, and before they knew it, they were back in beautiful, sun-drenched fields. Tilly followed Jack across a wooden stile and into a field of golden wheat, rustling in the gentle breeze.

"There it is," Jack said, pointing just ahead of them.

And what Tilly saw really could only be described as a crack in the sky. It was about two meters high, and looked like a rip in the fabric of the universe. On one side, the edge of the blue sky was flapping, like ripped wallpaper, and the other side looked like broken pottery with sharp edges. The crack was just wide enough for a fully grown person to squeeze through sideways, but the air was shimmery and translucent, as though there was a veil covering the gap, so it was impossible to see what was on the other side. Prince Charming's horse was standing next to it, tied to a fence post.

"What . . . ?" Tilly started. "Has . . . has that always been here?"

"Do you know, it's funny, when I try to think about when it arrived, I can't quite pinpoint it," Jack said. "It wasn't there, and then one day—it was. To start with, everyone was terrified, but some people have gone through it and most of them have come back."

"Most of them?"

"Yep," Jack said cheerfully. "But I guess some people might have just preferred what they found on the other side and stayed there. So what's the plan? I'll come through with you if you want."

"Are you sure?" Tilly asked, relieved. "I'd be very grateful."

"Of course," Jack said nobly, looking a little pale. "I can't just shove you through and hope you're okay. Do you want me to lead the way?"

"No, I'll go first," Tilly said, taking a deep breath.

It was a tight squeeze, and the sharp edge of the crack snagged on Tilly's jumper as she crouched down and edged through the gap.

"Oh," Jack said as he came through behind her. "It's just the same as home."

"You sound disappointed," Tilly said.

"Well, I am a little," he admitted. "You sort of hope for

something a bit more magical if there's a giant crack in the sky, don't you?"

"I'm just happy it's not more of that black emptiness," Tilly said, and Jack shuddered at the thought of what had happened to his friends' houses.

Where they stood was a great deal like where they had come from—green fields doused in sunlight stretched out in front of them under a vivid blue sky. Ahead of them was a hill with a very tall, thin tower on top.

"I guess that's where we're headed," Jack said, and Tilly nodded and set off.

As they climbed, it became clear that there was quite a commotion going on around the base of the tower. The sound of angry shouting and crying drifted down the hill toward them. Soon they could see that the ruckus was being caused by a gaggle of around fifty men, some of whom were teenagers—all gangly limbs and fresh faces—and some of whom were at least sixty, with one struggling in the long grass with a walking frame made of wood. All of them were at least moderately handsome, even the older ones, and dressed very expensively, and all of them looked extremely cross. As Tilly and Jack made their way up the last few meters toward the tower, one of the men stormed past in the opposite direction, trying to hide the tears streaming down his face.

"Excuse me," Tilly asked him gently. "What's the matter?"

"Daddy said all I had to do was come to this tower and call a certain phrase, and a pretty lady would throw her hair down for me to climb, and then I could marry her. And not only will she not let her hair down, but there are all these other princes here trying to marry her too!" He wiped his nose. "Are you trying to marry her?"

"Us?" Tilly said, confused. "Er, no."

"So, what, your dad just told you to come here?" Jack asked.

"Yes," he said. "He met my mum after locking her in a room and making her spin gold, and he heard on the grapevine about this tower/princess situation and thought it might be worth a try. But word has gotten out, and even though I was here first, all of the others are threatening to fight each other, and she won't even talk to us! She has to choose! And give us her hair ladder!"

"Does she have to choose?" Tilly asked.

"Why, of course she does," the man said, like Tilly had asked a particularly stupid question. "How else will she get rescued and married?"

"Well, actually . . ." Tilly started, but Jack pulled her away.

"I think we should go and see for ourselves," he said, and they left the prince sniveling in the field. They walked up to the base of the tower, where small, ineffectual scuffles were breaking out among the gathered princes. No one wanted to risk injury to themselves or their clothing. Some princes were still trying to call up to the window in the tower.

"Go on! Let down your hair! You promised!"

"I've got such a big castle! If you just come down, I can show you!"

"Don't listen to him! His castle has only got three stables!"

"My mother has a magic mirror you can borrow!"

And so it went on, and amid the chaos, Tilly and Jack searched in vain for Prince Charming and Oskar, as the shouting got louder and more desperate, until finally a head popped out of the window.

"Enough!" it yelled.

17

I Need to Come Up with a Better Story

Silence immediately fell among the princes, who stared up at the young woman glaring angrily down at the crowds.

"Will you all just please leave me alone?" she shouted. There was a further beat of silence, and then all at once the men started caterwauling again.

"Rapunzel, Rapunzel, let down your hair!" they shouted.

"No!" she yelled. "I don't even know any of you! Why would I let you climb up my hair?"

"So we can rescue you!" one prince shouted.

"And marry you!" another called.

"I don't know you!" she repeated. "I do not want to marry any of you! Also, I'm seventeen! I don't want to get married at all, let alone to someone older than my dad!"

"But princesses have to marry princes!" one more shouted. "It's how the story always goes!"

"Well, it's not how this story is going, I can assure you! I am making an executive decision to change my happily-ever-after. Now please go away!"

"Fine!" one prince said. "I'm leaving!" He started walking away very slowly. "This is your last chance! I'm really going! I'm very rich! And I won't be able to hear you change your mind if you leave it any longer!" The only answer was a banana skin that came hurtling out of the window and hit an entirely different prince in the face. The one who had been trying to call her bluff stamped his feet.

"I didn't want to marry her anyway," he said loudly, so the other princes could hear. "I'll get Daddy to find me a better one." And he turned on his heel and left.

"One down!" a voice echoed from the window. "I've got all the time in the world, and a lot of bananas."

It didn't take long for the princes to get bored once they realized Rapunzel was being entirely serious, and they started to disperse. Tilly scanned the crowd again, but there was still no sign of the original Prince Charming, or Oskar. And before long, there was only one prince left, sleeping curled up on the ground, sucking his thumb, everything having gotten a bit too much for him.

"Where on earth are they?" Tilly was stuck somewhere between exasperation and panic.

"We could ask her," Jack suggested, pointing upward.

Rapunzel was tentatively sticking her head back out of the window to assess the scene below, and spotted Jack and Tilly.

"Oh, you're still here," she said, sounding annoyed.

"We're not with them!" Jack called up. "We don't want to marry you! I swear! We're just looking for our friend. One of the princes kidnapped him."

"Ugh, they really are the most entitled, useless collection of people I've ever encountered," Rapunzel said. "Is there just one left?" She pointed to the sleeping prince.

"Yes. I'll get rid of him," Jack offered, and poked the prince with his toe.

"What? It wasn't me!" said the prince, spluttering awake. "Where's everyone gone?"

"I'm afraid it's all over, pal," Jack said firmly but kindly. "She's picked a prince and galloped off into the sunset with him, and everyone else has gone home. You'll have to go and find another damsel in distress."

"Ugh," the prince said, standing up and brushing down his over-the-top arrangement of lace ruffles. "Do you know," he said, "I'm not sure my heart's really in this catching-a-princess malarkey. I've always been ever so fond of Eliza, who works in the bakery in the village; she makes the most delicious bread, and we do make each other giggle. I might forget this princess thing and just see if she wants to grab a glass of mead sometime."

"I think that sounds like a really solid plan," Jack said,

clapping him on the back. "Maybe lose some of the ruffles before you ask her, though?" The prince smiled, and ambled off into the distance, talking about Eliza and her excellent cupcakes as he went.

"Coast is clear!" Tilly shouted up to Rapunzel, and she stuck her head out again.

"Cheers," she called. "I'll be right down!"

All of a sudden, a great torrent of tangled blonde hair was shoved out of the window and fell to the floor in an extremely matted heap, with twigs and moss and even what looked like a bird's nest caught in it. As Rapunzel hoicked herself out of the window and started climbing down the mess of hair, it became clear that none of it was actually attached to her head, and her real hair was cut into a sharp bob with angular bangs. She kicked out her feet and slid down the final few meters with a confidence that showed it wasn't the first time she'd exited that way.

"How do you do?" she said, smoothing down her dress. "I'm Rapunzel, nice to meet you. Thanks for helping clear out those princes. I owe you."

"You're welcome," Jack said, dipping into an awkward half bow and coming over all bashful.

"So you can come and go as you please?" Tilly asked, gesturing at the matted pile of hair.

"Of course," Rapunzel said. "I like to put word around that there's a wicked witch keeping me trapped to try to put all the princes off. I obviously misjudged, though—it actually seems to be yanking all the particularly annoying ones out of the woodwork. I need to come up with a better story. Or acquire an actual witch . . ." she said thoughtfully. "That'd put them off, thin out the crowd, you know. Anyway—you said you'd lost a friend? I get a pretty good view from up there. What do they look like?"

"Well, he's called Oskar and he's about the same height as me with brown skin and black curly hair," Tilly said. "And he'd be with a prince who looked a lot like all of the rest of them, but without the horse. The prince stole Oskar and took him to come and find you . . . which is why we're here. But they obviously didn't make it."

"Which direction did they come from?" Rapunzel asked.

"That way," Jack gestured. "Through the crack in the sky."

"The crack in the sky?" Rapunzel repeated, sounding confused. "What does that mean?"

"It's kind of hard to miss," Jack said. "It's a big old . . . well, crack in the sky, down at the bottom of the hill. You must be able to see it from the top of your tower. In fact, I'm kind of surprised we can't see it from here. . . ." He trailed off as he looked down the hill, where there was no sign at all of anything unusual.

"Will you show me?" Rapunzel asked, curious.

"Of course," Jack said eagerly.

"What about Oskar?" Tilly reminded him.

"We're looking for clues!" Jack said. "Something obviously went wrong between the crack and the tower, because we saw Prince Charming's horse left there."

"Fine," Tilly said. "But we have to find him before that blackness swallows anything else up."

"Sorry, what is swallowing what?" Rapunzel said. "I've obviously been in my tower for too long; I'm very out-of-date."

"I'll fill you in as we walk," Jack said as they set off, and began chatting animatedly to Rapunzel, with Tilly following a few paces behind. As they walked back down the hill, Rapunzel called nonchalantly to Tilly.

"Do watch out for the puddles," she said.

"What puddles?" Tilly said, confused both by the lack of any surface water, or indeed by the danger of puddles, should any exist. Rapunzel gestured to her left and Tilly looked and saw that there was indeed a puddle, not of water, but of . . . nothing. The same nothing that was behind the Three Bears' door, and in the Seven Dwarfs' house in the tree. It was more of the same negative substance, like a black hole: just a gap in the grass that was sucking light into itself and not giving anything back. You couldn't see the bottom of it, or any perceivable edges, either. It was just blank space.

"Do you know what that is?" Tilly said.

"I have no idea," Rapunzel said cheerfully. "It just appeared. A prince fell into it the other week and vanished. I was watching him leave from my window and he wasn't looking where he was going and then, zap, he was gone! So, I'd avoid touching it if I were you."

"Are there more of them?" Tilly asked.

"Not that I've seen," Rapunzel said. "Although I think that one is getting bigger."

"Totally normal thing to happen," Tilly said under her breath, moving away from the edge of the non-puddle. "Just a huge puddle of nothingness in the middle of a field, sucking princes into it."

The farther they got down the hill, the clearer it became that the crack in the sky was not where they had left it. There were just fields, trees, and sun, nothing out of the ordinary and nothing covered in sticky black liquid. Rapunzel eyed them as if she was beginning to regret following them.

"I swear it was just here," Jack said, looking around in a panic. "How am I going to get home?"

"Maybe it's just gotten smaller?" Tilly suggested, feeling

a little sick again. "Let's walk a bit farther in case we're in the wrong place?"

"No, it was definitely here," Jack said, pointing at the fence. "Look." They followed to where he was gesturing and there, flapping in the breeze, was a scrap of gray fluff caught on the fencepost. It exactly matched the color of Tilly's jumper.

"I promise there was something here," Tilly said to Rapunzel. "It looked like a rip in the fabric of the world. Maybe it's sealed itself over or something?"

"I'm not saying you're making things up," Rapunzel said, backing up the hill again. "I'm just saying—" But before she could finish her sentence, she was interrupted by a hoarse scream from somewhere nearby.

18

There's Never Only One Way Home

"Is someone there?" a voice shouted. "Help! Please, help!"

"Where are you?" Tilly shouted back. "We can't see you!"

"Tilly! Is that you, Tilly?" a different, even more desperate voice called. "It's Oskar! I have never been so glad to hear your voice!"

"Thank goodness!" Tilly said, a sense of relief washing over her. At least he was here, and alive.

"Where are you, mate?" Jack shouted again.

"I don't know!" Oskar called. "We can't see anything!"

The three of them turned around slowly, but there were no other living souls in sight, just fields and trees stretching out around them.

"Keep talking!" Rapunzel shouted into the emptiness. "So we can follow the sound of your voice!"

Oskar started shouting, "Tilly! Tilly! Tilly!" on repeat, and the first voice, which they assumed to be Charming, set up a steady wail of woe. They followed the shouts to the edge of the field, until it sounded as though they were right on top of the noise.

"Down here!" Oskar shouted.

"Pay attention!" Charming huffed, and they all looked down to see a hole in the middle of the grass, just a few meters ahead. In the bottom of the pit almost four meters down, were Prince Charming and Oskar, both looking incredibly cross and sticky. The edges of the hole were dripping with the same black substance that kept turning up all over the fairy tales.

Tilly's brain started working overtime. She felt like she had a box of jigsaw pieces but no time to lay them out neatly and put them together properly. And that was assuming they were all for the same puzzle in the first place.

"Tilly," Oskar said, "I thought I was going to have to spend the rest of my life stuck in this hole with this . . . this . . ." And Tilly could see him searching for and failing to find a suitable word to describe the prince. Oskar threw his hands up in frustration and just glared at Charming, who stuck his tongue out in response. Oskar looked up at Tilly in desperation.

"Look at what I've been dealing with."

"It's not my fault someone left a great hole in the middle of a field," Charming grumped. "Honestly, the King around these parts is clearly very neglectful when it comes to land upkeep." Everyone ignored him.

"How on earth did you end up down here?" Jack asked, peering nervously into the narrow pit opening.

"We came through that crack in the sky," Prince Charming said. "And had to leave my beautiful horse behind and walk. On my feet!"

"The walking wasn't the issue, though," Oskar said, rolling his eyes. "As soon as we came out of the other side, things started getting super weird. Nothing made any sense. The sky was flickering different colors, like a sunset on fast-forward, and we kept seeing people who disappeared—just disappeared—right in front of us. And then, out of nowhere, a wolf walked right up to us and asked if we knew where the three little piggies were, and then I tried to make a break for it to get back to you guys . . . and I didn't see the edge of this pit and fell straight in, and this guy just barreled straight in behind me."

"If my young squire had been looking where he was going—" Charming said.

"I am not your young squire," Oskar interrupted, in a voice that suggested it was not the first time he had reiterated this.

Rapunzel yawned. "I can't say I am particularly interested in why you're there," she said. "But these two are eager to get you back, so shall we focus on getting you out?"

"Can we find something to throw down?" Tilly asked, looking around.

"Fine, hang on." Rapunzel sighed, as if Tilly had been nagging her for hours. She stepped back, closed her eyes, and screwed her face up in concentration. At once her hair frizzed as if she'd rubbed a balloon on the top of her head—and then it started growing at an alarming rate. Before long it was down to the ground, and it kept growing and growing. Rapunzel opened her eyes and nodded in satisfaction before pulling a pair of scissors out of her apron pocket and hacking her hair off at the nape of her neck. With a practiced hand she tied a knot at the top to keep it together, picked up the hair-rope, and hauled it over the edge of the hole. Oskar shimmied up and over the side without much fuss, but Charming was looking at the hair rather distastefully.

"Go on, then," Rapunzel said. "We haven't got all day."

"Does this mean I can marry you?" Prince Charming asked hopefully. "That's how it works, isn't it? If I climb up your hair, I can marry you?"

Rapunzel rolled her eyes. "Unless you want me to leave you down there, I suggest you stop talking and climb," she said, bracing herself on her heels as Charming ungracefully scrambled up and onto the grass. Sweaty and sticky and rumpled, he went over to try to kiss Rapunzel's hand.

"Fair maiden, now that I have rescued you, I humbly ask—"

"Hang on there," Rapunzel said. "I literally just rescued you, you fool."

"Mere semantics!" Charming said, aiming for a signature charming grin. Rapunzel just yanked her hand away and walked off, leaving Charming in a huff on one knee.

"Oskar, let's go!" Tilly said, opening the book of fairy tales. "Now! Where are we?" She ran her finger down the contents page. "Okay, well, there doesn't seem to be a Rapunzel story in here." She swallowed nervously. "I'm not quite sure what that means. There's not even any mention of it in the contents."

"I think it means we're not in this book anymore," Oskar said quietly. "I have a horrible feeling that the crack was a sort of gateway between books. I mean, it's not from a story, is it? I've never read 'Jack and the Weird Sticky Rip in a Field,' at least."

"So what do we do?" Tilly asked. "Perhaps if we just read one of these stories, we'll go back there, right?"

"We could try," Oskar said. "But remember in the taxi on the way to the Inking Ceremony? Your grandma said it was dangerous to read yourself from one book to another, didn't she?"

"Yes, you're right," Tilly said, resigned. "That's definitely what she said—that it was like using a map when you don't know where you're starting from. I remember now."

"But do we have any other options?" Oskar asked nervously. "What's the worst that could happen?"

"Well," Tilly said, and began to list things on her fingers. "We could vanish from existence, or whatever happened to Jack back in the cottage could happen to us, or we could get stuck in some sort of eternal loop of this story, or we could just flat-out die horribly. Or we could get sucked into the Endpapers. . . . Hang on. . . ."

Tilly paused and tried to let her brain think everything through. "Okay, hear me out," she said slowly to Oskar. "Could we do what we did in *Alice in Wonderland*? Travel through the Endpapers into an Underlibrary?"

"Would we go back to London, though?"

"I don't think so," Tilly said. "There must be one in France somewhere, right? Presumably in Paris? And this is a book from a French bookshop. Or even if it's not there, I'd rather be stuck in real-life France somewhere than here."

"Okay." Oskar nodded. "I trust you. And I promise that I won't hold you responsible if we die gruesomely. Scout's honor."

"Are you even in the Scouts?" Tilly asked.

"Not the point, right now," Oskar said, holding his hand up in some approximation of what he thought a Scout's honor gesture might be, but ending up with something from *Star Trek*.

And with that he managed to break the mood and make them smile, just enough to give Tilly the courage she needed.

"Shall we say good-bye to them?" Oskar asked, nodding toward the fairy-tale characters.

"Well, Jack and Rapunzel at least," Tilly said.

Charming was sitting, sulking and dirty, on a rock, while Jack and Rapunzel were chatting and laughing nearby, ignoring him completely.

"So we're going to head off," Oskar said. "Thanks for helping us out."

"I hope you manage to get home okay, Jack," Tilly said.

"I think I've decided I'm going to stay here for a bit," Jack said, smiling at Rapunzel. "We might have some fun with some of these princes. Rapunzel needs a witch and I do love a bit of fancy dress. And fingers crossed the crack in the sky reappears, or I think of something else. There's never only one way home."

"What about me?" Charming wailed. "How do I get home! I don't even have a horse!"

"Why don't you see if you can find a stray prince?" Jack suggested kindly. "Maybe he can help, or take you home with him?"

"Oi!" Charming said, poking Oskar. "Are you sure you don't want a job as a squire? You weren't very good at finding the tower but maybe you could help me find my way home. Or at least to another castle. Or to another princess!"

Oskar just gave him a withering look.

"Do come and say hello if you're ever around these parts again," Rapunzel was saying to Tilly and Oskar. "If you do an owl hoot at the tower, we'll know it's you and I'll let my hair down. And you don't even have to marry me."

The four of them hugged, then Tilly opened the book of fairy tales to the last page.

"Okay, hold on tight," she said as Oskar took her hand and she read the last line, hoping her theory was correct.

19 ★

Some Truth to Every Story

Tilly and Oskar tried to stay calm as the shadows swaddled them and the fairy-tale lands faded away. There was a pause that seemed to last an eternity and then, suddenly, the darkness started to ease, like the first rays of a sunrise illuminating a bedroom. They began to make out the outlines of something physical and became aware of something definitively solid under their feet.

"Okay, well, we're somewhere," Tilly said. "As opposed to nowhere. Which is a good start." The light continued to brighten around them, and within seconds they were standing in a real room in between two desks, which were unfortunately both occupied by people staring in surprise at them. A slim, well-dressed man stood up abruptly, knocking over a glass of water in front of him.

"*Qui êtes-vous?*" he shouted. "*Dites-moi! Maintenant!*" The woman at the other desk was still just staring at them, mouth slightly ajar.

"Uh, *je ne . . . je suis anglais,*" Oskar stammered.

"You are English?" the man said in a heavy French accent, as if that explained several things.

"*Oui,* yes," Tilly said, relieved they could at least communicate in the same language. "I'm so sorry to, uh, crash into your office, like this. Could we just check where we are?"

"You are in la Sous-Bibliothèque de France!" the man said as if that should be obvious. Tilly sagged in relief. They were in an Underlibrary, and in France.

"So we're still in Paris?" she double-checked.

"*Mais oui,*" he said. "Where else would you be? You two are bookwanderers, obviously. That is how you say it in English, yes? But what are you doing just appearing in our office?"

"Are you in danger?" The woman spoke for the first time, and Tilly looked at her gratefully.

"No. Thank you," she said. "We just . . . we got stuck in a book." She tried an edited truth to test how it went down.

"Did you get to here from England?" the woman said, concerned.

"No, it's not that bad," Oskar explained. "We're staying in Paris and got stuck in a book we read here."

"That is good," the woman said. "Better than having traveled to the wrong country. And we are being rude! My name is

Colette Zhou, and this is Marcel Petit." The man nodded curtly.

"I'm Oskar," Oskar said. "That's Tilly. We came via the Faery Cabinet. Do you know it? It's Gretchen . . . Gretchen . . . What was her surname, Tilly?"

"You do not mean Gretchen Stein?" Colette said, looking worriedly at Marcel.

"Yes, her," Oskar said. "You know her?"

"Why, yes," Colette said. "Everybody here at the Library knows of her."

Marcel walked out from behind his desk and came toward them.

"You bookwandered from the Faery Cabinet?" he asked sternly, and all they could do was nod. "You must come with me straightaway."

"Stop, Marcel!" Colette said. "Wait for a moment! We do not know what has happened yet. Is it wise to take them upstairs before we have found more information?"

Marcel paused. "What do you mean?"

"How do you know Gretchen?" Colette asked, still much friendlier than Marcel.

"We don't really know her properly at all," Tilly said. "We just met her today. We're staying with Oskar's dad on holiday, and that was just the nearest bookshop, so we went there to bookwander."

"Okay, you see, Marcel," Colette said. "They are not working with her. She did not ask you to come here, no?"

"No, of course not!" Tilly said. "We didn't mean to come here at all! We just want to go home."

"Why would she ask us to come here anyway?" Oskar asked.

"It does not concern you," Marcel said. "We do not know who you are or if you are telling us the truth."

"My name is Matilda Pages," Tilly said. "I live in Pages & Co. in London with my grandparents—Archie and Elsie Pages."

"You are the granddaughter of Archibald Pages?" Marcel said, his hand dropping from the doorknob.

"Yes," Tilly said proudly.

"And you are a friend of the Pages family?" Marcel asked Oskar.

"Yes," Oskar answered easily. "Best friends, actually."

"You see! We can trust them!" Colette said, smiling at them warmly. She stood up and gestured to a small sofa at the back of the room. "Do sit down, and we can talk, yes?"

"Sure," Tilly said. "So do you know my grandad?"

"Oh no," Colette said. "But we have heard of him, of course, and how much he loves books and readers. You are very lucky to have him and to live in his bookshop."

"I know," Tilly said, and she did.

"I do not think he should have been asked to stop when . . ." Colette paused, and cocked her head to one side as she looked at Tilly. "You are Archie Pages's granddaughter?" Tilly nodded, knowing the equation that Colette was trying to do in her head.

"Your mother is his daughter?"

"That's how it usually works," Oskar said under his breath.

"My mum is Beatrice, yes," Tilly said.

"She is okay now?" Colette asked tactfully.

"Yes," Tilly said. Of course news of her mother trying to change a Source Edition had spread to other Underlibraries. "She's okay. . . . But, well, do you know about everything that happened with Enoch Chalk?"

"I am familiar with his name, I think. He works at the Underlibrary, *non*?" Marcel said. "But we have not had news of any problems with him here in Paris. Are there things that have been kept from us?"

"Oh," Tilly said, feeling awkward. "I don't want to get anyone into trouble, but he was the Reference Librarian in London and it turned out that he was . . . Well, he's a fictional character! He had escaped from his Source Book and been living in the real world for years, trying to find a way to make himself real. It was Enoch Chalk who trapped my mum in a book for twelve years to stop her telling people the truth about him."

"That is more horrible than I can imagine," Colette said, reaching a hand out and holding Tilly's. "She is back home now, though, you say?"

"Yes," Oskar said proudly. "We rescued her." Colette smiled warmly at him.

"And where is this Chalk now?" Marcel asked. "He has been put back in his Source Book and it has been bound?"

"Well, no," Tilly said. "He escaped and then no one knew where he went, and actually our Librarian, Amelia Whisper, lost her job for not telling anyone and trying to fix it all herself. Now the new Librarian, Melville Underwood, says he knows where Chalk is and is going to bring him back. But he's actually awful and not helpful at all, and he wants to stop children bookwandering. . . ." Explaining it all out loud made Tilly realize just what a mess everything had become.

"It is terrible to hear of what is happening at your Underlibrary," Colette said. "We have heard some rumors and I do not like the sound of this Underwood man at all. We shall have to tell our Librarian and he can speak to him officially."

"I did *not* get a good vibe from him," Oskar said vehemently.

"You have met him?" Colette said in surprise.

"Yes," Tilly said. "We went to his Inking Ceremony the other day. . . . Well, it was only the day before yesterday, I suppose. He was very friendly when he did his speech, but then he spoke to us afterward and told us that he wants to stop children bookwandering!"

"And he wants to start binding books," Oskar said. "He said people should have to ask permission every time they want to bookwander."

"It is disgusting!" Marcel said. "It should not be allowed. What is being done to stop him?"

"Not much," Oskar said. "Lots of librarians seem pretty keen on him. There was all this talk of protecting British bookwandering, and stuff like that, and everyone was clapping away."

"It is not how it should be," Colette tutted. "It makes me scared for what is to come."

"Who is your Librarian?" Tilly asked. "Can they do anything?"

"A wonderful man named Jean-Paul," Marcel said. "We are very fortunate to have him here. He would never keep information like this from other Underlibraries."

"And you are from a bookwandering family too, Oskar?" Colette asked kindly.

"Yeah!" Oskar said proudly. "I actually am! My grandmother is Clara Roux!"

"Ah, dear Clara!" Colette said. "I do not know her well, but I have met her. She is a very talented artist, no? We have some Source Editions of work she has done in our stacks."

"Cool," Oskar said, enjoying having his family member be of note for once.

"But, hang on," Tilly said. "You like her, but she is friends with Gretchen, and you don't like *her*, it seems. Why were you so worried when we said we had bookwandered from Gretchen's shop?"

"Because she will not do what she is told!" Marcel said. "She makes a mockery of the Underlibrary!"

"She does not think that we do a useful job here," Colette said more calmly. "She does not like that the Underlibrary has rules. She will not register her name or her bookshop with an Underlibrary, and she lets people do as they please in her bookshop and her books. Rumor has it that she has had many love affairs in books, but"—she paused and blushed—"I should not discuss such things with children. Gretchen believes all the rules will create people like your Underwood man. Maybe she is more right than we think, with what you say about your Underlibrary."

"No," Marcel said firmly. "There is not that way or her way only. Gretchen is just as dangerous as Melville Underwood, but in different ways. I do not agree with either of them. There is no place for these extreme points of view. There must be a middle way."

"But I would not like to have someone like Underwood in charge of us here," Colette said.

"You would rather have Gretchen Stein?" Marcel said.

"I do not know." Colette shrugged. "She loves stories in a way he does not, I believe. And she does not want to be in charge, and I think that is important. It is rare that the people who want to be in power are the best people to do it."

"But what about the people who are even higher up and more important? Like the Archivists?" Tilly said. "Do you think we could ask them to come and get rid of Underwood?"

Colette narrowed her eyes. "Perhaps," she said quietly.

"Of course not!" Marcel said loudly. "No one has heard from the Archivists, not even a tiny whisper, for I think two hundred years. Perhaps they no longer exist, or maybe they never did and are just a myth, a fairy tale. Do you not think past Librarians have tried to speak to them when things are difficult? They are just a story to provide hope."

"So you don't think they're real either?" Tilly said sadly.

"I do wish that they were," Marcel said, a little more gently. "But there is no evidence of them, only stories. The legend goes that there is a map that would take you to them, but it is only a myth, an adventure story for baby bookwanderers. I do not think it would be sensible to put your faith in the Archivists at this time."

Tilly felt utterly deflated, realizing that some part of her had believed that someone would swoop in and fix everything that was going wrong, before it got any worse.

"But . . ." Colette said, and looked at Marcel, who shook his head abruptly.

"But what?" Oskar pushed.

"But there is some truth in all stories," Colette said. "And our history is not just a foreign country, but a road to where we are today."

"Now," Marcel said. "Enough riddles. You two must answer a few more of our questions and then we will decide whether to take you to talk to our Librarian or to deliver you home. Which book were you in?"

"We started in this one," Tilly said, holding out the book gripped in her arms.

"Fairy tales," Marcel said. "Who told you this was a clever idea?"

"Gretchen said we . . ."

"Of course, I forget, it is Gretchen at the root of this story," he said. "Of course she told you it was safe to go here. Imagine sending children into the fairy-tale lands on their own."

"It wasn't so bad," Oskar said, a little defensively. "There was some seriously weird stuff, though."

"Yes?" Colette asked.

"Some of the stories seemed to have gotten, well, lost, I suppose," Tilly said, unsure of how to describe it. "There were places that stories, or characters, were supposed to be, and there was just blank blackness stretching out into infinity. Hang on, look. . . ." She turned up the page where the Three Bears' story was supposed to be and showed them the blank pages. "You see, there's just a gap."

"May I?" Colette asked, holding a hand out for the book, and Tilly nodded, passing it over.

"There are many stories missing," she said, flicking through. "Where did you visit?"

"Well, we were definitely in 'Jack and the Beanstalk,'" Oskar said, but when Colette looked up Jack's story, she frowned before holding it out to show them. It was now blank as well.

20

It's the Journey, Not the Destination

"Where is Jack? What's happened?" Tilly said, panicked.

"Maybe it's disappeared because Jack came through into the new book with us?" Oskar suggested. "And when the crack vanished, he couldn't get home?"

"A crack that vanished?" Marcel repeated.

"Yes, it was a big old crack in the sky," Oskar said. "We went through it and we think that's why we ended up in the wrong book."

"You see, you say it was not so bad, but you found yourselves in the wrong book, *non*?" Marcel said. "And you ended up here? How did you do that? That is not the way it is supposed to work."

"We got here through the Endpapers," Tilly answered without thinking.

"But that is not how it should go," Colette said, looking intently at Tilly. "If a reader goes into the Endpapers, they could be lost for a long time. How did you get to here? That is what happens to the fictional people, not you."

Tilly shrugged and tried to put a convincingly confused look on her face. "I don't know," she said. "My grandparents said fairy tales have different rules, so isn't it because of that?"

"Perhaps," Colette said thoughtfully. "They are strange places after all. And getting stranger from what we hear. It is not so good to hear that stories are getting lost, and there are cracks in the sky."

"We also saw a character seize up and explode, and then a new version of the same person walked in the door," Oskar said.

"And a puddle of nothingness, just in the middle of a field," Tilly added.

"A puddle of what?" Marcel repeated. "I do not understand this word."

"I don't know how to explain it better," Tilly said. "It was like just . . . nothing. A black hole. And Rapunzel said that a prince disappeared into it."

"Prince Charming?" Marcel said. "When was this?"

"No, a different prince. We were with Prince Charming," Tilly said.

"Well, not our Prince Charming," Oskar chimed in. "They're all called Prince Charming, aren't they?"

"He is right," Colette said. "Many of them are. It is just, we had a lost Prince Charming fall into our Endpapers last week. We put him back in his right place, but he said that he was just walking and then suddenly he was here. I wonder—"

"Something is not right," Marcel interrupted. "Fairy tales were always dangerous, but this is different. We will write down what you have said for our records, and we will make sure that you get home safely. Where does your father live, Oskar?"

"We need to go back to the Faery Cabinet first," Oskar said, "and give Gretchen this book back, and then we can go home. It isn't far from the bookshop, so we'll be fine from there. Thank you."

"We shall get you a car," Marcel said. "Follow me."

Marcel talked continuously about the history of the French Underlibrary as they left the office and walked along a wide corridor. "You will see when we come up higher that we are underneath the old site of the National Library, on rue de Richelieu, in the center of Paris. We are close to the Louvre museum, where the *Mona Lisa* painting lives. In 1996 most of the library's collections were moved to a new building by the river, but we decided to stay here and make the most of some of the vacated space. And so here we are."

He pushed open a set of double doors and they found themselves in a huge domed atrium, not dissimilar to the British Underlibrary main hall. But instead of big arches looping from one side of the ceiling to the other, the French equivalent had a series of domes painted in cream with golden decorations and lights at the very apex to create the illusion of windows. The edges of the domes descended to the floor in narrow cream-and-gold columns that didn't look sturdy enough to hold up such an expanse of ceiling. Wooden spiral staircases curled up the sides of the walls, leading to the highest points of the bookshelves that lined every wall of the vast room.

"What do you think?" Marcel asked them, glowing with pride.

"It's beautiful," Tilly said.

"Yes, the most beautiful Underlibrary in the whole world," Marcel said, and Tilly couldn't argue.

Once they were out on the streets of Paris, Marcel soon managed to flag down a taxi, and Tilly and Oskar slid into the back seat. After a quick word with the driver, and some euros passed through the window, Marcel came to the back door and bobbed down into a crouch to speak to them.

"He will take you back to the bookshop," he said.

"Thank you so much for helping us," Tilly said. But as Marcel carefully shut the car door, Colette rushed out onto the street, pink-cheeked from running up the stairs.

"Wait!" she said, out of breath, and Tilly rolled the window down. "I have a gift for you." She passed Tilly a brown paper bag. "Do not look now—I will be embarrassed. It is just a very small thing, something that you might find useful if you ever feel as though you are lost and searching for a new path." Marcel looked at her and frowned, but Colette just smiled and patted his arm.

"Well," Marcel said through the car window. "I feel that maybe there is more to your story than you have shared with us today, but I believe and hope that I am right that this is for good reasons. Perhaps do not tell Gretchen what you have told us about the fairy tales, and, Matilda—you should ask her about her time at the British Underlibrary and see what she says. Stay safe, *mes amis*." Tilly and Oskar nodded, a little nervously, as Marcel knocked gently on the roof of the car and it pulled off, wheels crunching in the snow.

It was not a long drive back to the Faery Cabinet, and looking at Oskar's watch, they realized that they had only been gone for about forty-five minutes of real-world time.

"I'm not sure I'll ever get used to the way time works in books," Oskar said.

"And who knows how it works in fairy tales?" Tilly added. "For all we know, it might have taken negative time being in there, and if we hadn't gone to the Underlibrary we would have come out before we went in!"

"I can't even begin to think about that right now," Oskar said. "Anyway, what did Colette give us?"

Tilly opened up the bag and pulled out a ball of red yarn, and a very thin pamphlet titled "A History of Libraries."

"Well, I don't know what I expected but it wasn't that," Oskar said. "Is it a joke?"

Tilly was bemused and a little disappointed. "She said it would help us if we got lost. I don't understand." She flicked through the pamphlet, which was in very small, smudgy type, and seemed to be exactly what it said on the front.

"Bookwanderers really do love speaking in riddles, don't they?" Oskar said, rolling his eyes. "Why can't someone just say something straightforwardly for once? Couldn't Colette have said, 'Here, Tilly and Oskar, it is a ball of red thread. It may be useful for tying things together or wrapping presents.' And I think she's overestimated even your interest in libraries with that booklet. It looks extremely boring."

"I'll save it for a rainy day," Tilly said. "And you know librarians love all that sort of stuff. Clues and riddles and 'it's the journey, not the destination'—all those things people say in stories. They want us to work it out for ourselves."

"As always," Oskar said.

Tilly went to put the red thread and the pamphlet in her pocket and realized that it was already full. She pulled out the little cloth bag of bread crumbs.

"What's that?" Oskar asked.

"Hansel and Gretel gave it to me," she said, staring at it. "When Jack and I were looking for you. We bumped into them in the forest."

"I always miss the good bits," Oskar complained. "Anyway, how did you get it out? I didn't think we could take stuff out of books?"

"I don't think we can," Tilly said, looking in confusion at the bag in her hand.

"Maybe just a fairy-tale thing?" Oskar said.

Tilly shrugged and didn't reply. *Another jigsaw piece that doesn't fit*, she thought.

Moments later, they pulled up outside the Faery Cabinet and found Gretchen and Clara chatting away over cups of coffee, seemingly unconcerned as to where Tilly and Oskar had gotten to.

"There you are!" Gretchen said as they walked in, but she didn't seem worried at all. "Where did you guys go in the end?"

"Well, we started in 'Little Red Riding Hood,'" Tilly said, trying hard to sound very casual. "But we ended up on a bit of a detour."

"I see." Clara smiled, but there was a question in her eyes. "Where have you come from?"

"The French Underlibrary," Oskar said, and Gretchen looked bemused.

"But . . . how?" Clara said.

"Through the Endpapers," Oskar answered happily, before Tilly dug him in the ribs with her elbow, trying to remind him that they weren't supposed to travel that way.

"I think we can trust Mamie," he said, blinkered by his excitement over his newfound bookwandering heritage.

"Trust me about what?" Clara said.

"Nothing," Tilly said, trying to sound nonchalant. "It's just that we ended up in a different version of the fairy tales and so the book chucked us back to the Underlibrary—just a precaution-ary thing. Like you said, no harm done!"

"But you ended up at the Underlibrary via the Endpapers?" Gretchen repeated, looking curiously at Tilly.

"Yep, but you know, fairy tales!" Tilly said. "Unpredictable!"

"So what did you make of the Underlibrary, then?" Clara asked, letting Tilly move the conversation on.

"It was beautiful," Tilly said, relieved. "Everyone was very friendly and helpful."

"Were they now," Gretchen said grumpily.

"They said you'd say something like that," Oskar said, which made Clara laugh.

"Why do you dislike the Underlibraries so much?" Tilly asked.

Gretchen sighed. "I just can't think of anything worse than being subject to the whims and rules of a huge organization that wants to control and monitor my behavior. I disagree on principle."

"But we need some rules, right?" Tilly said uncertainly.

"Do we need more rules than what common sense dictates?" Gretchen pushed back. "Do you think there were Underlibraries when people first realized they could bookwander?"

"When even was that?" Oskar asked.

"We do not know for certain," Clara said. "A long time ago."

"I believe that people have found themselves inside stories for as long as stories have been told," Gretchen said. "But the Underlibrary and the Librarians, why, that is a much more recent invention."

"But not all librarians are like that," Tilly said. "Both of my grandparents were librarians, and they wouldn't want it to be like that."

"It's hard to properly know the people we love," Gretchen said.

"Come now," Clara said to her, a note of chastisement in her voice.

"What do you even mean by that?" Tilly said, feeling a little cross. "You said you didn't know them. I know them, and they are not like you're saying. They believe in all the same things as you. Anyway, you're obviously British from your accent, so are you claiming you never met them, that you've never had anything to do with the British Underlibrary? My grandad was Librarian when you would have found out you were a bookwanderer, so how come you don't know him?"

"Tilly," Gretchen said, not quite able to meet her eye. "There's something I need to tell you."

"What a surprise," Tilly said under her breath, feeling as though she was skirting around quicksand whenever she was talking to Gretchen.

"I do know your grandparents," Gretchen said.

"So you lied," Tilly said shortly.

"Gretchen!" Clara said. "You did not tell me!"

"So how did you know them?" Tilly said. "And why did you keep it a secret?"

"Well, if we're being honest, I used to be best friends with your grandmother."

"I don't understand why you would lie about that," Tilly said, feeling wrong-footed and deceived.

"I, too, am interested to know this," Clara said.

"I wanted to be able to get to know you properly first," Gretchen said, trying to sound breezy. "I didn't want you to ask them about me before you'd heard my side of things!"

"That doesn't sound good," Oskar said.

"Your grandma and I worked together at the British Underlibrary for several years," Gretchen said.

"You're the woman she worked with on the fairy-tales research?" Tilly said, the pieces clicking into place in her mind. "The one she used to be friends with?"

"Yes," Gretchen said. "And see, you've already heard the story! This is why I didn't say anything! I dread to think what they've told you! They'd definitely forbid you from coming here. I'm sorry. I panicked when I realized who you were."

"So what happened with you and Elsie?" Oskar asked. "She didn't even say anything mean about you! We just knew she'd worked on a project in fairy tales with someone and that you'd disagreed on what to do with the information you had."

"Yes," Gretchen said. "But give me a minute to get some coffee brewing, and then let's go back to the beginning."

* 21 *

A Book Will Welcome Any Reader

"I grew up in England," Gretchen said, hands wrapped around a steaming cup of coffee. "In the north Yorkshire countryside. I didn't realize I could bookwander until I was an adult. I was working in a university library and I yanked Brutus out of *Julius Caesar* into the stacks with blood on his hands; I nearly had a heart attack. Thankfully, one of the other librarians was a bookwanderer and realized what had happened, and we had a day trip down to the Underlibrary, where I was offered an apprenticeship and then a job. I loved doing the most dangerous work I could find, and so I joined the research department, exploring unpredictable and out-of-print books, or books with multiple versions or strange histories. I loved it. You never knew what you would be doing or where you would be going from one day to the next.

"After a few years I was paired up with Elsie, and we clicked immediately. Your grandma is a brilliant woman, Tilly, and the combination of my fearlessness and Elsie's brain meant we made a great team and were given one of the Underlibrary's most exciting projects: finding out more about fairy tales. But it was pitched to us as a project to help us understand them. Yes, to create some maps that meant bookwanderers could explore them more safely, but I didn't realize that the bigger picture plan—which we hadn't been told—was to try to work out why fairy tales behaved differently, with a view to forcing the usual rules on them. Elsie and I spent a good year exploring and mapping, and learning about the beautiful wildness of these stories, but, unbeknownst to us, everything we were learning was being analyzed and used against the stories. When we found out, we protested, but were ignored. They wanted us to go into the stories to try to bind up some of the boundaries, to keep all the stories and characters in place. It was the final straw for me and I quit."

"But surely Grandma didn't agree with all of that?" Tilly said.

"No, I don't think she did," Gretchen said. "But she thought that the way to stop them was to work with them and convince them from inside."

"That sounds very sensible," Oskar said, earning him a hard stare from Gretchen.

"It does!" he maintained.

"Well, Elsie did what she thought was right, and so did I," Gretchen said. "And I believe firmly that everyone should be free to follow their own path. I have no issues with the Underlibraries existing. I just don't agree with their insistence on all bookwanderers registering with them and on forcing them to be subject to their rules. I made my views clear, but I was happy to simply retreat, and yet that wasn't good enough for the British Underlibrary. They insisted on withdrawing me."

Clara gasped. "Gretchen! I did not know!" she said, putting an affectionate hand on her arm.

"What does that mean?" Oskar asked.

"Withdrawing is an antiquated process that bars someone from an Underlibrary," Gretchen said. "I am not permitted to enter the British Underlibrary, as I am classed, ridiculously, as some kind of threat. I'm not sure if you are aware, but no one can take away your ability to bookwander, so it means very little, really, as I have no interest in ever going there again. It's symbolic nonsense."

"I've heard some people talking about binding books to stop people bookwandering," Tilly said, choosing her words carefully so as not to give too much away, remembering Marcel's warning about Gretchen. "What does that mean? Can they do that to you?"

"Books aren't interested in who is reading them," Gretchen said. "A book will welcome any reader any age, any background, any point of view. Books don't care if you can understand every word in them, or if you want to skip bits or reread bits. Books welcome everyone who wants to explore them, and thankfully, no one has worked out a way to stop that. Of course, humans meddle, and at some point in bookwandering history, a bothersome librarian realized that books could be bound entirely, and that way you could stop anyone from bookwandering in them. They can still be read like normal books, but there's no way to get inside."

"It is a barbaric idea," Clara said.

"It's not fair!" Oskar said, outraged all over again at the thought.

"It is what I have been trying to show you," Gretchen said. "The Underlibrary does not care about fair. It cares about power."

"That's what Grandad said," Tilly remembered.

"Well, I always thought he wasn't so bad," Gretchen said. "When Elsie started going out with him, I did think she could have chosen a lot worse from among the ranks of librarians."

"Do bookwanderers often marry other bookwanderers?" Tilly asked, curious.

"Well, no, not always," Gretchen said. "But there is a reason bookwanderers often fall in love with each other. It is a big thing to share together—or not to share."

"What about falling in love with fictional characters?" Tilly asked quietly, thinking of her mother.

"Why, yes," Gretchen said, without a pause. "It would be madness to pretend that doesn't happen. I have had several beautiful romances with fictional characters. I've been taken out to dinner by several iconic heroes and heroines in my time."

"But were you in love with them?" Tilly pushed, knowing that her own mother had been head over heels for Captain Crewe inside *A Little Princess*. "Were you ever tempted to stay with them?" Oskar shot her a warning glance.

"I can't say I was," Gretchen said. "I was too fond of my

life here. But I believe people should be able to make their own decisions about such things. You have to make peace with either living inside a book forever or knowing you can't really ever build a real life with the fictional person you're in love with. The Underlibrary is so hung up on just outlawing any romantic relationships—but how is it that different from the friendships we form with fictional characters, really?"

"Yes, but I wouldn't want to go and live in *Anne of Green Gables* forever," Tilly said. "However much I love being friends with Anne."

"And most people would agree with you," Gretchen said. "But don't you think that people should be allowed to make up their own minds?" She looked directly at Tilly. "And is it right to stop people if they aren't causing any harm to anyone else?"

"I . . . I'm not sure," Tilly said. "What if they were leaving behind people who needed them? Just hypothetically speaking."

"Well, I would say, hypothetically, that it is up to every person to decide what they are willing to sacrifice, and what is worth making sacrifices for. But whatever they decide, they should not be punished for it by a group of people who claim to have their best interests at heart, but are far more focused on trying to control bookwanderers."

"Do you think the Archivists would punish people?" Tilly asked. "If they're out there somewhere?"

"I think the Archivists are there to help," Clara said. "They are not a literary police force."

"So you believe they are real?" Tilly said.

"Yes, I believe they exist," Clara said. "I think who they are, and what they are for, depends on what you are asking them. I think that they are perhaps buried in stories, hiding, or being hidden. Or just waiting for the right moment, *peut-être*. I would be disappointed after all this time to find they are no more real than these fairy tales." She smiled at Tilly but was distracted by a huge yawn from Oskar.

"I think it's time to get you two home," Gretchen said.

"How is it only the afternoon?" Oskar yawned. "I need a nap."

"You two are always welcome at the Faery Cabinet," Gretchen said as they wrapped themselves in coats and hats and scarves and headed back into the gentle snowfall. "And, Tilly, I am assuming you will tell your grandparents about your adventure. Please remember we have all simply acted according to the principles we hold to be right and true in situations where there is no clear path." And with that she closed the shop door, and the three of them wandered home, Oskar arm in arm with Clara.

"Did you have a good morning?" Gabriel asked as Tilly and Oskar wearily climbed the stairs and flung off their winter clothes.

"Uh-huh," Oskar murmured. "Very busy, need to sleep."

"I thought you just went to a bookshop?" Gabriel said, looking confused. "Why on earth are you so tired?"

"Maybe the fresh air?" Tilly said, trying to be polite. "Or the traveling, bit of jet lag?"

"I'm not sure you get jet lag from London," Gabriel said. "But I guess you've had busy days, and are still recovering from school finishing. You two have a nap, and I'll bring you up some Orangina in an hour?"

"Thanks, Dad," Oskar said, dragging his feet upstairs.

"*Merci*," Tilly said. "I'm sorry."

"Nothing to apologize for," Gabriel said, watching them head upstairs with a perplexed look on his face. "Sleep well."

22

A Plot Hole

Gabriel roused them gently an hour later, and Tilly felt discombobulated in that way that going to sleep in the light and waking up in the dark always confuses your brain.

"I think you should get up now," Gabriel said softly. "Otherwise you won't sleep tonight. Do you want to come downstairs and we can plan what to do for dinner?"

"Thank you," Tilly said. "Do I have time to call my grandparents first?"

"Yes, of course," Gabriel said. "Just don't fall back asleep!"

"I promise." Tilly smiled and picked up her phone, steeling herself for the conversation ahead.

They picked up on the third ring.

"Tilly! How are you!" her grandma said. "We're missing you so much!"

"I'm good," she said, trying to sound cheery and non-suspicious.

"What have you two been up to today?" Grandad chimed in.

"Visited any galleries? Eaten any particularly excellent croissants?"

"Um, not quite," Tilly said. "We went to that bookshop, and chatted with its owner, who turned out to be a bookwanderer after all!"

"Oh, lovely!" Grandma said. "Who was it?"

"Gretchen Stein?" Tilly said nervously, and there was a moment of silence on the other end of the phone.

"Okay," Grandad said slowly. "And . . . did you mention us?"

"It's okay, we don't need to skirt around it," Tilly said. "I know who she is."

"Right," Grandad said, still speaking very slowly. "What did she say exactly?"

"Please don't worry if she said anything too alarming," Grandma chipped in nervously. "About when we worked together. Her perspective is obviously a little different from ours!"

"Don't worry," Tilly said. "She's didn't say anything horrible. In fact, she was really quite nice, and way more worried about you saying nasty things about her."

"Did you go bookwandering with her?" Grandad asked.

"Not with her," Tilly said, which wasn't a lie.

"I'm so glad," Grandma said. "Since we asked you not to bookwander in Paris."

"When I say we didn't go with her . . ." Tilly said in a small voice.

"Ah," Grandad said. "Okay. Well, I'd be lying if I didn't say I'm a little disappointed, Tilly."

"I know," Tilly said, her guilt crashing up against a distinct sense of indignation. "But Gretchen and Clara said . . ."

"Clara said what?" Grandma said, confused.

"Oh yes," Tilly said. "That's the other thing—Oskar's mamie is a bookwanderer too!"

"Oh," Grandad said. "Well, that certainly explains a lot! So, where did you go?"

"A book of fairy tales," Tilly said nervously. She saw no point in lying.

"Matilda!" Grandma said. "After everything we'd said."

"I know, but Gretchen and Clara said that we were sensible enough to go, and we were in the bookshop, so they knew where we were!"

"It's not about you being sensible, Tilly," Grandma said. "It's about fairy tales being dangerous. We're not telling you stories to scare you for the sake of it—these are real concerns. It's a miracle you managed to get out safely. I'm not sure if it's better or worse that Gretchen wasn't with you. You did have Oskar there, though, yes?"

"Yes—and you can trust us! We're not little kids who can't look after themselves. Even when things went wrong, we just worked it out!"

"What went wrong exactly?" Grandad said, and Tilly cursed herself for mentioning that anything had gone awry.

"Just some small stuff," Tilly said, trying to play it down. "Like, Oskar fell in a hole. Just normal stuff."

"A hole? How did he fall in a hole?!"

"It was a bit weird," Tilly admitted. "It was like a sinkhole in the middle of the field, and it was all sticky."

"It wasn't a plot hole, was it?" Grandad said, sounding worried.

"A what?" Tilly said.

"Sounds like he fell into a plot hole," he repeated. "Did anything confusing happen beforehand?"

"Actually, yes," she remembered. "He did say that the sky changed color, and something else, something about a character appearing and disappearing."

"Almost definitely a plot hole," Grandad said. "Did you get him out okay? He hasn't started speaking strangely and not making sense?"

"Could that have happened?" Tilly said anxiously.

"Yes!" Grandma said, struggling to keep the frustration from her voice. "What we told you about fairy tales wasn't for our own entertainment."

"But anyway, he's fine. Rapunzel let him climb up her hair," Tilly explained. "He didn't even hurt himself; he was just really dirty from all the black gunky stuff we kept seeing everywhere. Is that stuff normal in plot holes?"

"Firstly, yes, that would be normal. A plot hole is a story caving in on itself," Grandma explained. "So a bit of book magic will leak out. But you said you saw it everywhere, not just in the plot hole?"

"Yeah," Tilly said. "It was like, well, sort of like ink, I suppose, or oil. It was in the plot hole, but also there when . . . Oh yeah, we met Jack, as in Jack and the Beanstalk—who was really nice—but at one point he sort of froze up and then exploded, and there was the black stuff under him there."

"I've never heard of a character exploding before," Grandad said, and Tilly could hear him put his hand over the phone, and talk quietly to Grandma so Tilly couldn't hear.

"Anyway he was fine too," Tilly said. "Well, until . . . until his story vanished."

"What?" said Grandma and Grandad in unison.

"Well, when we came back out, from a different story, the pages were just blank!"

There was more muffled talking.

"Did you see it anywhere else?" Grandad asked.

"We saw bits and pieces of it around," Tilly said. She decided not to fill them in on the crack in the sky, or the visit to the French Underlibrary, until they started giving her some answers, not just grilling her for information and then speaking so she couldn't hear them. "But why? Book magic isn't a bad thing, is it?"

"Well, it is if it's leaking out in stories. It shouldn't just be oozing out everywhere," Grandad said. "It's a valuable resource, and what fuels bookwandering, so something is going wrong if it is just spilling out. Do you still have the book you traveled into?"

"No, it's back at Gretchen's," Tilly said. "It's from her shop, the Faery Cabinet."

"On that subject, we don't want you going anywhere near that shop again," Grandad said.

"You don't let me do anything!" Tilly exploded. "I'm not allowed to bookwander, I'm not allowed to go to a bookshop. And what are you even doing back at home to sort it all out? Gretchen may be . . . eccentric, but at least she talks to us and trusts us, and lets us make our own decisions about things!"

"That's hardly fair," Grandad said. "And look what happened when Gretchen let you do what you wanted."

"What happened?" Tilly said, with an anger in her voice that she'd never used with her grandparents before. "That we were allowed to explore? That some bad stuff happened, but we dealt with it and everyone is fine? That we found out something about book magic that seems to be useful? Which of those things is the problem exactly?"

"Tilly, you don't sound like yourself," Grandma said. "This isn't how we expect you to talk to us. We're only trying to keep you safe."

"Well, maybe I should just sit inside not speaking, or doing anything at all, so I'm perfectly safe all the time?" Tilly said, trying to fight back frustrated tears. "And what if neither you or Gretchen are right? Have you thought about that? Maybe Gretchen isn't the safest bookwanderer, but look at how all the rules have turned out in the British Underlibrary! Look at what Underwood is trying to do!"

"Melville isn't a good representation of what most librarians or bookwanderers think," Grandad said.

"But everyone was clapping and cheering for him, and

they've let him be in charge, and it only seems to be you and Amelia and Seb who don't think he's right," Tilly pointed out.

"I'm sure that we aren't the only ones," Grandad said. "But people want to keep their jobs, and some of them are trying to change things from within—like Seb."

"That's what Gretchen said you wanted to do, Grandma," Tilly said, feeling as though they were talking in circles.

"Well, yes," Grandma said. "She's right, I did, but that was a specific situation a long time ago. I felt that I could convince the Librarian at the time that we needed to protect fairy tales. . . . But that was then, Tilly, and this is now. Things change."

"Yes, they do," Tilly said mutinously. "Anyway, I have to go now. We're going out for dinner with Oskar's family."

"Well, we're all really looking forward to having you home, sweetheart," Grandma said. "And please don't—" But Tilly, even though her heart was hurting, put the phone down before Grandma could finish the sentence. The phone seemed as though it were glaring at her accusingly as she pressed the red button.

"They were just going to tell me what not to do," she said out loud, trying to justify herself.

"Who are you talking to?" Oskar said, poking his head around the door. "You've spent too long in books if you're narrating your own life." And Tilly smiled, despite herself, and took a deep breath. She'd deal with Grandma and Grandad when she got home.

That evening the family headed downstairs to a small, cozy bistro in the square. They ate mussels cooked in white wine, garlic, and herbs, with great chunks of crusty bread and salted butter. Tilly had never eaten mussels before, but she quickly got the hang of using the shells of one to pinch out the next one, and even got used to the unusual slippery texture.

Over dessert of crème brûlée with a sugary top that splintered with the most satisfying of cracks, they exchanged Christmas gifts. Tilly bashfully gave Gabriel and Marguerite a coffee-table book about artists and writers who had lived and worked in Paris, ignoring the tug on her heart she felt when she thought about Grandma spending ages helping her choose it, and all the other presents, at Pages & Co. For Clara they had picked out a cloth-bound edition of *Madame Bovary*, the French classic, which earned an approving nod. And from Clara, Oskar and Tilly were both given identical rectangular-shaped gifts, which they unwrapped to reveal leather-bound notebooks embossed with their names. Oskar's was a deep ruby red, and Tilly's a forest green, and on both, their names were picked out in gold capital letters.

"Oskar, yours is for you to draw in,"

Clara said. "It brings me such pleasure that you have inherited my love of art, and I know that you think you are not so good, but it runs in your blood, *chéri*," she said with what was as close as Clara would ever get to a wink. "And this is for you to practice. To draw whatever you imagine: Paris, fairy tales, maps, maybe. And, Tilly," she went on. "I know how much you love other people's stories, and I wonder if you have ever thought about writing your own? And so here is space for you to try, if you wish. I think that you might have a story to tell one day, Matilda."

"Thank you," Tilly said, stroking the smooth cover. "It's the nicest notebook I've ever had. I'll save it for something special."

"Although a desk full of empty notebooks does no one any good," Clara said. "Do not wait too long for something special to present itself. Go out and find it."

For the rest of the frosty evening they talked about books and school and music and Paris and Gabriel and Marguerite's art gallery; and Tilly realized that, much as she wouldn't trade bookwandering for anything, this bubble of calm and happiness felt like a welcome rest from the uncertainty of whatever was going on at the British Underlibrary. She sat back in her chair, letting the feeling of sleepy contentment wash over her, as Oskar and his family chatted animatedly around her, and the snow fell gently outside the windows.

23

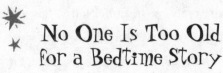

No One Is Too Old for a Bedtime Story

The wonderful sense of normality stretched into the beginning of the next day as well, and Tilly tried to push her argument with her grandparents to the back of her mind. She didn't even text them, determined to show that she wasn't a little girl anymore and could look after herself.

After a breakfast of croissants with Nutella and fresh strawberries, Marguerite, Oskar, and Tilly bundled up tightly against the cold and set out into Paris for a day of "being tourists," as Marguerite put it. The apartment was only a few streets away from the huge glass pyramid of the Louvre, and they posed for photos, pretending they were touching the top of it. They walked past the long lines snaking around the building.

"The best time to go," Marguerite said conspiratorially, "is at night. It is open until nearly ten o'clock on some evenings, and it is quite magical to wander around. Also, the *Mona Lisa* does not have quite so many people taking selfies in front of it. You must come back, Tilly, and we can visit."

They crossed the huge courtyard and wandered along the Tuileries Gardens, which were almost out of a fairy tale themselves. Ornate streetlights and neatly tended hedges dusted with snow turned into broad pathways lined with trees, which were spindly and sparkly in the frost. There was a man valiantly selling ice cream and even some people who were buying it. The three of them drank hot chocolate, ate dainty pastel-colored macarons, and stopped for a ride on a merry-go-round, where their hands froze to the poles, even through their gloves. They were the only riders as it spun around and cranked out its traditional cheery song. Cheeks pink, and heart full, for a few moments Tilly forgot about broken fairy tales and Melville Underwood and her mum's sadness and her grandparents trying so hard to protect her she felt smothered. She spun around and around, snowflakes settling in her eyelashes, and only Paris mattered.

As they walked back to the apartment, Tilly felt the pleasant glow of happiness and the tiredness that came from a good, busy day, like being wrapped in a heavy but comforting blanket. She was surprised at how sad she felt about leaving the magic and mystery of Paris, not to mention the exceedingly good hot chocolate.

Even more disconcertingly, she found that she also felt a sense of loss thinking about not seeing Gretchen again. Gretchen seemed so sure of who she was, and just carried on being herself, regardless of what anyone else said or did. Tilly felt as though she kept having to make big decisions about who she was and what she believed in, when she didn't really know either of those things. She felt herself tugged in too many directions, and feared that she was going to be pulled into nothingness.

Too quickly, and in a flurry of good-bye hugs and kisses, as well as a few quickly wiped-away tears, Tilly, Oskar, and Gabriel were making their way back to the train station. Their journey from only two days ago was done in reverse; the trip to the buffet car was just as unsatisfactory, and the scenery rolled by as before. The only difference was that Tilly left Grandma's book of fairy tales firmly in her backpack.

At St. Pancras station, Grandma, Bea, and Oskar's mum, Mary, were waiting on the platform, and Tilly felt an overwhelming sense of home wash over her, despite that awful last phone conversation with Grandma and Grandad. She stopped herself from giving in to the instinct to run over to Grandma for a hug and just said a formal hello, clearly confusing Bea, who stepped forward and wrapped Tilly up in a hug that made it hard to breathe, not that Tilly cared at all.

"I'm so glad you're back," Bea whispered into Tilly's hair. "Mum and Dad said you had quite the adventure while you were there. I missed you so much." Tilly felt something inside her unclench a little bit, something that she hadn't even realized she was keeping tensed, and she snuggled further into Bea's coat, which smelled of peppermint and paper and a little bit of moth-balls, as though it had been at the back of a cupboard for a long time.

"So, I hope you two aren't sick of each other," Grandma said, looking at Tilly and Oskar.

"Uh, why?" Oskar asked, confused.

"Well, because we've invited you and your mum to come and spend Christmas with us," Grandma said, smiling.

"For real?" Oskar said, looking at his mum and grinning. "How come?"

"Well," Mary said. "Archie and Elsie and I were just

chatting about plans, and I mentioned that we didn't usually do a turkey for just the two of us and they insisted there was space for us at Pages & Co.!"

"Christmas is about all kinds of families," Grandma said. "The ones we're born into and the ones we make."

"But I don't have presents for anyone!" Tilly said, stricken.

"Well, I think we might have a few books around you can choose from." Grandma smiled.

"Amazing." Tilly grinned at Oskar, glad she would have an ally around. "Christmas at the bookshop is the best."

Tilly walked with her mother back through the doors of Pages & Co., and was pleased that coming home felt like slipping into a perfectly temperated bubble bath. The moonlight spilled in through the windows, lighting the spines of the books silver. Without thinking, Tilly found herself searching for her mother's hand, and Bea took it as if it was the most natural thing in the world as they walked through the shop toward the kitchen door. Before they got there, Grandad emerged, grinning, despite everything.

"Tilly!" he shouted, and met them halfway, pulling Tilly into a big hug. "We are so glad you're home, sweetheart. We love you very, very much. And perfect timing—dinner is ready!" And indeed, delicious smells were wafting through the kitchen door, and Tilly realized how hungry she was. The six of them settled around the kitchen table, and Grandad put down a huge toad-in-the-hole, its batter golden and steaming. Apparently yesterday's arguments had been forgotten, and Tilly wasn't sure if she was relieved or frustrated.

"Sausages from the butcher up the road," Grandad was saying. "I thought I'd make something properly English to welcome you back, Tilly!" He served it up into generous portions, alongside green beans and caramelized onion gravy that pooled satisfying in the toad-in-the-hole. They talked about everything but bookwandering, as Mary was there, and after sticky toffee pudding and vanilla ice cream, which Tilly could barely finish, both she and Oskar were struggling to fight back yawns.

Grandma and Grandad had already sorted all the sleeping arrangements, so Tilly pushed her chair back and, after a round of good-night hugs, headed up to bed. She started unpacking but was far too exhausted, and so the only things that made it out of her bag were the most precious items: Grandma's fairy-tale book, the bag of bread crumbs, the red yarn, and the "History of Libraries" pamphlet from Colette. After making sure they were safe, she put on her coziest pajamas and snuggled into bed, toasty warm from a hot water bottle placed there by someone earlier. She was just about to turn her bedside light off when there was a soft knock on the door.

"Are you too old to have a story before bed?" said Bea, popping her head around the door. "I don't mind who does the telling."

"No one is too old for a story before bed," Tilly said.

24

  No Rules for Reading

"What do you fancy?" Bea asked, looking at Tilly's heaving bookshelves. Her attention was caught by the collection of curiosities Tilly had put on top of her bookcase for safekeeping. She picked up the pamphlet. "'A History of Libraries . . .'" she read from the front. "This looks . . . dense. Did you pick it up in Paris?"

"Uh-huh," Tilly said vaguely.

"And the rest of this stuff too?" Bea said, looking at the fairy-tale book, the red yarn, and the little bag of crumbs in confusion.

"Nope," Tilly explained. "The book is Grandma's; I borrowed it. And the yarn was a gift, I guess, from a librarian in Paris. She's actually the one who gave me that pamphlet. And I . . . accidentally brought the little bag home from a bookwandering trip."

"You took it out of the book?" Bea said, surprised, and Tilly nodded.

"Was I not supposed to?" Tilly bristled a little, not wanting another telling-off.

"I don't really care about supposed to," Bea said, with something that looked a lot like a grin playing across her face. "But I'm pretty sure it shouldn't be possible. How did you bring it out?"

"It was an accident," Tilly said. "I just had it in my pocket and forgot about it, and when we wandered out again, it was still there. But how is it different from you bringing your bee necklace out?"

"Do you know, I hadn't thought of that before now," Bea said. "I suppose it could be because it's not something mentioned in the text of the book? Or, more likely, considering what you've just told me, it might be because I was pregnant with you when I left. How curious. Maybe don't mention it to your grandparents just yet. They will definitely worry about it. Will you tell me if it happens again?" Tilly nodded at her mother in happy surprise. "I know they were hard on you for bookwandering, Tilly, but remember that after what happened to me, they just want to keep us all safe." This was the first time that Bea had mentioned her ordeal so casually, just as a matter of conversation. As soon as she realized what she'd said, something darkened in her face, and she slipped back into that almost-being state she'd been stuck in since she returned. But even a glimpse of the real Bea was hope enough for Tilly, especially the whisper of a promise of a future ally and confidante. Bea went back to looking at the pamphlet.

"You said a librarian gave this to you?"

"Yes, but I don't think it's good bedtime reading," Tilly said. "It's a history of libraries with really small type."

"Maybe not for now, then," Bea agreed. "But perhaps you'll find it interesting to dip into someday." She flicked through the pages, and as she did, out fluttered a small piece of paper. On one side, in spidery handwriting, it read "The path to freedom starts at 20540." There was nothing else that she could see. Bea held it up to Tilly.

"Had you seen this?"

"Nope," Tilly said, getting out of bed and coming to look at it.

"'The path to freedom . . .' I wonder what it means," Bea said slowly, brow wrinkled in concentration. "It's not enough numbers for a date, or a time. . . . Hang on," she said after a few moments. "Do you know what a zip code is?" she asked Tilly, who shook her head.

"It's what Americans call postcodes," Bea explained. "It's five numbers, just like this. Of course, it might not be anything to do with that. It could just be a random doodle from way back when."

"Would you be able to work out where the zip code was for, if it was that?" Tilly asked.

"Let's have a look," Bea said, pulling her phone out of her jeans pocket and typing in the five numbers. "Well, if it is a zip code, then it's for Washington, DC, in America. And specifically the Library of Congress. Oh, and look! The address of the library is 101 Independence Avenue. . . ."

"The path to freedom!" Tilly said, pointing to the spidery handwriting on the scrap of paper.

"Yes!" Bea said, looking triumphantly at Tilly. "It seems like it's an address for the Library of Congress. It is a pamphlet about libraries, so I suppose that's not so surprising."

"Have you been there?" Tilly asked. "To the Library of Congress?"

"No, I haven't," Bea said. "But it's supposed to be very beautiful."

"Do you think that's where the American Underlibrary would be?" Tilly said.

"Yes, I believe it is," Bea said. "Oh, and look." She peered closely at the other side of the piece of paper. "There's something else, written in the crease. More numbers and letters. Your eyes are probably better than mine." She passed the piece of paper to Tilly, who held it up close to her face.

"PN," she read out loud. "6110649, I think, and then another 1, or maybe 2, that's smudged, so I can't read it." Bea tried typing the number into Google, but it brought up no results at all.

"Is it a phone number?"

"Maybe," Bea said. "It could be something to do with the Library of Congress, I suppose, if this note really does mean something—which it might not. Who did you say gave you this?"

"A librarian called Colette," Tilly said.

"And was she a regular librarian, or an Underlibrary librarian?"

"Underlibrary."

"I wonder if she was trying to tell you something?" Bea mused. "Did she say anything else?"

Tilly racked her brain. "I can't really remember," she said. "She said . . . something about being lost? Or getting home? It was all a bit cryptic."

"Librarians." Bea rolled her eyes. "Never just come out and say what they mean."

"Do you think you'll ever go back to the Underlibrary?" Tilly asked.

"Ah, I'm not sure," Bea said slowly. "I think maybe bookwandering isn't for me anymore. It makes me feel very anxious at the moment—the thought of going back into a book. Bookwandering is never going to be something simple and fun for me now. When I met your father, everything changed."

"Would you have done it differently?" Tilly said, not able to look at Bea when she asked. "You know, if you could do it all over again?"

"No," Bea said immediately. "Everything that happened led us here, and here is where I want to be. We've had a funny old journey, full of much more hardship than I would have ever predicted, or welcomed, but we have each other and we have your grandma and grandad, and we have Pages & Co. We have our family and our friends and our stories, and so we are not doing too badly however you look at it." She paused. "I know the last few months have been strange, for both of us—having to get to know each other. But, Matilda"—she took Tilly's hands tightly in her own—"never doubt that I love you very much, or worry that I want to be anywhere else but here, with you. And right now, I want to be sitting in bed, reading a book together. How does that sound?" She squeezed Tilly tight. "Go on, choose anything you like."

Tilly noticed one of her favorite comfort reads, *The Secret Garden* by Frances Hodgson Burnett, the same author who had written *A Little Princess*.

"Is this okay?" she asked Bea.

"Yes, of course," Bea said. "Are we starting at the beginning?"

"Let's skip the sad bits," Tilly said, happy to speed through the tragic opening of the book where a young Mary Lennox is sent to live at the isolated Misselthwaite Manor after her parents die. "Let's read the bit near the end once they've already found the garden—it's my favorite part. When everything starts getting better."

"That sounds like an excellent plan," Bea said. "There are no rules for reading, after all."

Tilly snuggled up in bed with Bea, and even though it took a little bit of fidgeting to find a position that was comfortable, they soon found a natural way to fit together, with Tilly nestled into the crook of Bea's arm. Tilly flipped through the book, past Mary discovering the abandoned and dying garden, right through to when Mary, with her cousin Colin and their friend Dickon, started growing it again. Tilly and Bea took turns reading the book out loud to each other, but when it was Tilly's turn, something curious started to happen.

"There is Magic in there—good Magic, you know, Mary. I am sure there is."

"So am I," said Mary.

"Even if it isn't real Magic," Colin said, "we can pretend it is. Something is there—something!"

"It's Magic," said Mary, "but not black. It's as white as snow."

They always called it Magic and indeed it seemed like it in the months that followed—the wonderful months—the radiant months—the amazing ones. Oh! the things which happened in that garden! If you have never had a garden, you cannot understand, and if you have had a garden you will know that it would take a whole book to describe all that came to pass there. At first it seemed that green things would never cease pushing their way through the earth, in the grass, in the beds, even in the crevices of the walls. Then the green things began to show buds and the buds began to unfurl and show color, every shade of blue, every shade of purple, every tint and hue of crimson. In its happy days flowers had been tucked away into every inch and hole and corner. . . . Iris and white lilies rose out of the grass in sheaves, and the green alcoves filled themselves with amazing armies of the blue and white flower lances of tall delphiniums or columbines or campanulas.

As Tilly read out loud, entirely absorbed in the story, Bea glanced up and held in a gasp of wonder as a carpet of lush green grass seemed to roll out from under Tilly's bed, covering the floor in springy freshness. And as she watched, flowers and buds sprouted from behind bookshelves and cupboards, and the scent of summer billowed through the room. When a robin flew out of nowhere and settled on the bedframe, and started whistling a tune, Tilly was startled out of the book.

"What . . . ?" she said, a little scared by the garden that was growing in her bedroom.

"Keep reading!" Bea whispered, and so Tilly did.

The seeds Dickon and Mary had planted grew as if fairies had tended them. Satiny poppies of all tints danced in the breeze by the score, gaily defying flowers which had lived in the garden for years and which it might be confessed seemed rather to wonder how such new people had got there. And the roses—the roses! Rising out of the grass, tangled round the sun-dial, wreathing the tree trunks and hanging from their branches, climbing up the walls and spreading over them with long garlands falling in cascades—they came alive day by day, hour by hour. Fair fresh leaves, and buds—and buds— tiny at first but swelling and working Magic until they burst and uncurled into cups of scent delicately spilling themselves over their brims and filling the garden air.

And what she read came to be all around them, until the bed was like a boat in a river of flowers. They were surrounded by plants of all kinds and colors, both those described in the book and many more besides them.

Roses and sunflowers and tulips
and flowers they didn't even know
the names of stood **tall** around them,

and vines wove themselves up the walls, and around the delicate trees that were lining the room, their graceful branches reaching up in arches for the vines to follow.

"Am I doing that?" Tilly asked, reaching out and touching a rose flowering by her head.

"I think you must be," Bea said, looking at her daughter in amazement. "I always knew you were magical."

"Is this a sort of bookwandering?" Tilly asked.

"I suppose so, but how extraordinary . . ." Bea said in amazement. "We're obviously not inside the book. You've brought it out to us."

"Is it . . . Is it because I'm not normal?" Tilly said warily. "Because I'm half-fictional? When I was on the train to Paris," she said, remembering, "there was a moment when I was reading Grandma's book of fairy tales, and I thought I saw a forest coming inside the train, but no one else could see it. Do you think that was something magical, like this?"

"Firstly, normal is overrated," Bea said. "This is clearly something rather special. And I imagine that whatever happened on the train is the same sort of thing. And yes, it must have to do with you having one foot in each world." Bea's eyes were full of light and joy and wonder as she stared at the room, full to bursting with sweet-smelling plants. "What a gift," Bea said, kissing the top of Tilly's head. "Maybe there's a little beauty left in bookwandering, after all."

25

Whose Magic Is It Anyway?

The next morning, Tilly woke up hot and gasping for air. Her dreams had been full of twisting vines, and sickly-sweet blooms, and people hiding behind trees, and she was relieved to find herself in her own bed in her own home. Bea was already gone from the camp bed on the floor, where she was sleeping due to the full house, and Tilly glanced at the clock on her bedside table and realized that it was already past ten a.m. on Christmas Eve. Even stranger than waking up late on Christmas Eve was the fact that next to her clock lay a large brass key that she had never seen before. She picked it up, and as she turned it over, her thumb felt something soft in its intricate crevices. There was a bit of very fresh mud stuck there.

"I don't think you're supposed to still be here," she said, and put it with the yarn, the bag, and the pamphlet so she could ask her mother about it later on.

Tilly made her way downstairs to find Amelia Whisper sitting at the kitchen table with her grandparents. Everyone had rather unfestive, thunderous looks on their faces, and in the middle of the table was a small pile of leaflets, one of which Grandad was waving around angrily.

"How on earth is he getting away with this?" he was saying. "Oh, hello, Tilly. Good morning." He put the leaflet back and smoothed his jumper down.

"What's that?" she asked. The Underlibrary's logo and motto were printed in the top corner of the leaflet, and below them was a list of seminars. They included "Whose Magic Is It Anyway?," "Books Are a Resource, Not a Retreat," and "Protecting Children by Protecting Books."

"Melville is on a propaganda mission," Grandad said angrily. "Dressing up his prejudice and his schemes in respectability. Having a seminar on something doesn't make it right."

"Hello, Tilly," Amelia said, shooting a glare at Grandad and standing up to give her a hug. "How was Paris?"

"It was . . . interesting," Tilly said unsteadily.

"Elsie and Archie told me you had quite the adventure in some fairy tales?"

Tilly nodded. Of course they had shared it with her. They told Amelia more than they told her these days.

"Have you gotten any further working out what's going on?" Tilly said a little pointedly.

"It's complicated," Amelia said, either not noticing or not minding Tilly's tone. "It would seem as though someone is taking advantage of the instability in fairy tales to draw out book magic, and of course, our minds are naturally going toward Melville, considering his sudden arrival and rather wanton use of processes that require book magic. But we don't have any physical proof of that to convince the librarians, so Seb is keeping an eye on him as much as possible. Even with this nonsense"—she gestured at the leaflets—"he's not doing anything technically wrong, or anything we can use to demonstrate he's the one behind the leaking book magic."

"Is he traveling into fairy tales, do you think?"

"Well, we don't know," Amelia said.

"Can't we stamp him?" Tilly asked.

"Well, you're not allowed to stamp someone without their knowledge," Amelia said.

"But Chalk did it to me!" Tilly said angrily.

"But we can't sink to his level," Amelia said.

"Okay, well, has he found Chalk yet? Tilly asked, changing the subject. "He said he would. Is anyone checking what he's doing to find him? Is anyone actually doing anything?!"

"It's only been a few days, Tilly. Calm down," Grandad said. "And remember, your grandma and I can't bookwander anywhere without Melville knowing, and Amelia is under intense scrutiny at the Underlibrary. We have nothing to go on with Chalk. It's a wild goose chase, and a waste of our efforts if Melville is already on it. Let's focus on the bigger picture."

"Melville says he's personally looking into the Chalk situation," Amelia said. "And I believe him. It's embarrassing for him to have a Source Character just lost somewhere. He won the vote on his promise to retrieve Chalk, so he'll be prioritizing it for sure, to keep everyone on his side."

"Let's all remember that it's Christmas," Grandma said. "We gain absolutely nothing by ruining our holidays worrying about things outside our control. The Underlibrary is closed for a few days now, and we have Mary with us, so let's just all try to relax and celebrate."

"You're right, Elsie," Grandad said. "Now, Amelia, what are your plans for Christmas?"

"Actually, I'm staying in London for Christmas. It's just me this year," Amelia said.

"Well, we'll lay a place for you here tomorrow!" Grandad said excitedly. "If you'd like?"

Amelia only hesitated for a moment.

"That would be absolutely lovely, if you're sure it's no trouble?" she said.

"Not at all," Grandad assured her. "The more the merrier! We have a turkey that would feed a small country, so you'd be doing us a favor."

Tilly couldn't take it anymore. How were they all just

carrying on as if nothing was happening? Talking as though whether there was enough turkey to go around was the biggest problem they were facing. As if leaking book magic and Chalk *and* Underwood getting up to goodness-knows-what were minor trivialities.

"So that's it?" she interrupted, her voice louder than she'd expected it to be. "We're just going to wait and see? Great plan." And she turned on her heel and left the room, leaving her family in quiet shock.

Christmas Eve was always busy and exciting at Pages & Co. The shop was open until the afternoon for people in search of last-minute Christmas presents, and it was a flurry of wrapping and finding and fetching. Tilly usually loved getting involved, but even though she threw herself into helping at the shop, she couldn't wholly take her mind off how frustrated she was with all the adults around her. But there was a magic in helping people find the perfect book for someone they loved, and the Christmas spirit finally got into her bones.

Tilly made her way to the back of the ground floor to find Jack, who ran the bookshop café. Predictably it was as busy as the rest of Pages & Co. and full of shoppers sitting down in relief, sipping coffee or mulled wine, and nibbling at one of Jack's festive treats. Tilly spotted peppermint brownies sprinkled with crushed-up candy canes, sugar cookies topped with marshmallows made to look like melting snowmen, and plenty of traditional mince pies.

"Can't stop! Help yourself . . . within reason!" Jack called when he spotted her. Tilly grabbed a brownie, and headed up to the children's floor.

There she helped an overwhelmed grandmother pick out a selection of books for her various grandchildren, pointed a harried-looking dad toward the copies of *The Gruffalo*, and fielded an unusual request for a book about Rasputin. When the clock struck four, the last shoppers were ushered out with their brown paper bags and totes printed with the *Pages & Co.* logo. The shop was tidied, the sign turned to **CLOSED**, the Christmas staff given hugs and mince pies, and there was a chorus of "Merry Christmas," then the Pages family, together with Mary and Oskar, tumbled, exhausted, back into the kitchen to start preparing dinner together.

"Tilly, would you mind just going and double-checking that the main door is locked?" Grandad said as he chopped up a butternut squash. Tilly, slightly grudgingly, hopped off her chair and headed into the dim bookshop—where she walked smack into an out-of-breath Gretchen.

26

Looking in the Wrong Places

"What are you doing here?" Tilly said in surprise, as Gretchen caught her breath.

"Tilly, hello!" Gretchen said, as if it were the most natural thing in the world for her to turn up on their doorstep on Christmas Eve. "The door was open, so I just came in."

"Do Grandma and Grandad know you're coming?" Tilly said.

"Not exactly," Gretchen admitted. "Are they through there? Could you let them know?"

Tilly wasn't sure what else to do but turn around and go back into the kitchen. She walked through and stood looking at Grandma, Grandad, Bea, and Mary, who were chatting away as they cooked.

"Are you okay, sweetheart?" Grandma said, noticing her standing there.

"Yes," Tilly said. "But . . . well, Gretchen is here."

"Gretchen?" Grandad said as his face went a little paler underneath his whiskers. Grandma stood up so quickly her chair fell backward loudly, and Tilly and Oskar followed her out into the bookshop to see the two women staring at each other as though they were looking at ghosts. Gretchen took a half step toward Grandma, who held her hand out as if to shake hands and then changed her mind and withdrew it just as Gretchen reached hers out.

"Just hug already," Oskar said. And so they did.

"Do you want a cup of tea?" Grandma asked, because sometimes, in these situations, the best and indeed only thing to do was to offer a cup of tea.

"A coffee would be lovely," Gretchen said. "It's been a bit of an arduous journey."

"Well, it is Christmas Eve," Grandma said. "Which is a funny time to visit anyone, let alone your estranged best friend whom you haven't seen in, what, thirty years? More?"

"Well, it's important," Gretchen said. "Meeting Tilly made me realize that."

"You're very welcome here," Grandma said. "Sincerely, Gretchen, even after all these years, it is good to see you." And Tilly could see Gretchen's shoulders relax a little at Grandma's words. "Come in and get comfortable and we can talk."

"Thank you," Gretchen said. "I know it's a lot to find an extra bed on Christmas Eve."

"An extra bed?" Grandma repeated.

"Well, it's an awkward time of year to find somewhere to stay," Gretchen said. "And you know what it's like running a bookshop in this day and age. Funds are tight and all. So I had hoped there might be a spare sofa or corner I could tuck myself into."

"Right, of course," Grandma said, masking her surprise. "I'm sure we can figure something out."

After an awkward dinner of small talk, and Mary being told that Gretchen was an old work friend of Grandma's, which was true after all, Bea went upstairs with Mary and Oskar to help sort out the sleeping arrangements.

"Will you go and help, Tilly?" Grandma asked.

"I want to stay and talk," she said.

"We just need a minute to ourselves first," Grandad said, but Gretchen immediately raised an eyebrow.

"I don't see why Tilly can't stay," she said. "After all, she's involved, isn't she? And what she and Oskar saw in the fairy tales is useful information."

"See, Gretchen thinks I can be helpful," Tilly said.

"It's not that we don't think you're helpful, sweetheart," Grandad said. "We just need a bit of time to catch up."

"I don't have anything I can't say in front of Tilly," Gretchen pushed, earning a hard stare from Grandma.

"Tilly, go and help with the beds," Grandma said firmly. "Now, please."

Tilly shoved back her chair and stomped out of the kitchen, but she couldn't resist lingering behind the door, listening to what was going on inside.

"We can start by asking why you allowed Tilly and Oskar to bookwander inside fairy tales in the first place," Grandad said, as soon as he thought Tilly was gone.

"Because they are young bookwanderers with their own hearts and minds, and clearly with their wits about them," Gretchen said. "It isn't for me to tell them where they can or can't go."

"But fairy tales, Gretchen," Grandma said.

"Elsie, we do not share the same opinion on fairy tales. Yes, they're wilder than some stories, but if you don't mess with them, then they won't mess with you."

"That's naive, and you know it," Grandad said.

"And yet here they both are, safe and sound," Gretchen said. "And the fact remains that they were able to provide us with valuable insight as to the structural discord inside the fairy tales. Which is why I'm here. I'm not merely after a slice of Christmas pudding, I assure you. I want to help you work out what is going on. You may not like to admit it, but, Elsie, between us, there aren't many people who know more about fairy tales."

"But why the sudden change in allegiance?" Grandma asked. "We've been on opposite sides of this debate for decades."

"Ah, you make it sound so dramatic," Gretchen said. "It's not like there's a war happening, or if there is, then it is us versus whatever is going on at your precious Underlibrary."

"There's no need to be snide," Grandad said, clearly finding it harder to forgive and forget than Grandma did.

"Archie, if anyone is swapping sides, it's you," Gretchen said. "I've always said the Underlibraries have too much power, and now you're on the outside as well."

"Regardless," Grandad said, realizing she had a point and not wanting to dwell on that for too long, "I'm still not sure our motives or goals are aligned enough. Elsie and I don't want to topple the Underlibrary—we just think that Melville Underwood is not the best person to be running it."

"To be honest, I couldn't care less about what happens to the Underlibrary," Gretchen said. "As long as they don't bother me, I won't bother them. I've lived outside their rules and regulations for years now, and I'm very content to carry on like that. My concern is making sure that whatever is happening in fairy tales is stopped."

"Well, that we can agree on," Grandma said. "But why now, Gretchen? What couldn't have waited until after Christmas?"

"I have reason to believe that something worse is about to happen," Gretchen said. "Something I think you might be able to shed more light on."

"This better be good," Grandad said.

"I went bookwandering in a few of my collections of fairy tales yesterday, after what Tilly told us," Gretchen explained. "And things are even more extreme than last time I visited. I wandered into several books and witnessed a number of characters in the wrong stories.

"There were twelve disgruntled princesses in dancing shoes who had teamed up and gone rogue—they were hunting down princes and imprisoning them. There were two wicked stepmothers fighting over who was the most beautiful in the land. But there were also wastelands of stories with no characters left, not to mention all the gaps and holes everywhere I already knew about. And worst of all, there was book magic leaking out everywhere.

"So I started asking around to see if any of the characters had an idea of what was going on. Many of them said they had seen a tall stranger with a cane wandering around and watching them, or asking unusual questions. And that reminded me of what Tilly told me about the shenanigans at the Underlibrary, and the man who had gone missing. . . ."

"Tilly told you about Enoch Chalk?"

"Yes, that was his name!" Gretchen said.

"And you came all the way to London to tell us that?" Grandad said. "You couldn't have sent us an email? Picked up the phone?"

"I thought I might be able to help," Gretchen said. "You know, like the old days. What do you say, Elsie?"

Tilly left them discussing Chalk and Underwood and the messy tangle of things going wrong, and headed upstairs, where she was presented with an armful of blankets and pillows by Bea.

"How do you feel about a bookshop sleepover with Oskar?" she said. "We're a bit cramped up here."

The new sleeping arrangements left Mary and Bea sharing

a room while Gretchen was going to take Tilly's. It used to be a treat for Tilly to be allowed to sleep in the bookshop, and she'd choose somewhere snug and make a duvet nest to hide away in, reading long into the night with her flashlight. But it felt a bit different doing it because she'd had to give her bed up on Christmas Eve.

"Come on, I'll help," Bea said, and led the way down the stairs.

"Do you like Gretchen?" Tilly asked suddenly, as they headed to the children's section.

"I'm not sure I've said more than ten words to her since she arrived," Bea said. "So I haven't had much of a chance to form an impression yet."

"Grandma and Grandad don't like her," Tilly pushed.

"I'm not sure that's fair," Bea said. "I don't think it's a case of liking or not liking. I think that they've taken very different approaches to a lot of things in the past, and also shared a lot of big life experiences, and that they're not sure yet if they trust her. What do you make of her?"

"I . . . I like that she treats me and Oskar like real people," Tilly said eventually. "She let us decide for ourselves whether we wanted to go bookwandering in her shop, and she didn't give us a load of rules."

"And you feel like your grandparents do?"

"Yes," Tilly said vehemently, as she piled up blankets in one corner for her, and Bea did the same for Oskar nearby.

"But Gretchen and your grandparents have very different jobs in your life," Bea said. "I don't doubt that Gretchen thinks very highly of you—who wouldn't? And she wouldn't put you in danger on purpose. But Grandma and Grandad know you better than anyone, Tilly, and they would put you first over every single other thing in this world. I think you know this deep down."

"Yeah, I know," Tilly said. "I do. But don't you think that maybe Gretchen is right about some things?"

"Like what?"

"Like, that there are too many rules, and that the Underlibrary is doing too much meddling, and people should be left to decide on their own about how they want to be a bookwanderer?"

"I think that a lot of what Gretchen says is interesting," Bea said.

"She believes in the Archivists, you know," Tilly said. "And Grandad and Grandma don't. They said they were just a story. But I don't understand why we can believe in some stories and magic, but not the Archivists? Why are they less real than Alice or Anne or Sara or . . . my dad!"

"Well," Bea said slowly, as if it was hurting her to say it, "you know that those people aren't real in the same way we are? They exist in many ways, but not outside their own stories."

"So why can't the Archivists be like that?"

"What do you mean?"

"People talk about them as if they have to be people like us or not exist, but why can't they be something in between? We spend so much time in the in-between; I'm an in-between person! Maybe people are just looking in the wrong places."

Bea nodded. "And maybe people should be listening to you a bit more," she said. "Tilly, I think you might be onto something."

27

The Meaning of Life

Once everyone else had gone to bed, Tilly and Oskar were still up chatting about Gretchen and the Archivists when they heard someone downstairs. Creeping back down to the ground floor of the bookshop, they found Gretchen rustling around in the books.

"I'm so sorry to wake you," she said. "I was just looking for something to read."

"Do you need any help?" asked Tilly.

"I'm okay, thank you. I found something that caught my fancy," Gretchen said, holding up a blue hardback. "And I shall try very hard not to crack the spine so as not to cause your grandfather more anxiety."

"Okay, then," Tilly said. "Good night. Merry Christmas."

"Tilly," Gretchen called after them. "I hope it hasn't caused you unnecessary stress, me turning up like this. I didn't mean to make it difficult between you and your grandparents. I am trying to help, you know."

"I know," Tilly said.

"I imagine it must be frustrating for you," Gretchen went on. "Having to hang around while the adults make a plan. I'm sure they'll come up with something soon."

Tilly shrugged. "If they haven't done anything by now, they'll probably just wait until Melville does something awful they can use as evidence. But by then it will be too late," she said.

"Well, I hope they don't have to wait too long for him to put a foot wrong," Gretchen said. "I bet there's all sorts of evidence out there if you look in the right places."

"Like where?" Tilly said, although Oskar was already shaking his head.

"Well, look at how much you two found out from one quick trip to some fairy tales," Gretchen said. "You found a plot hole, and were the ones who realized that book magic was leaking out, which meant your grandparents could connect the dots with Melville. And I know that you were instrumental in working out what that Chalk man was doing. You've clearly got an eye for clues. I'm sure you could find something quickly . . . if you were allowed to help more."

"We are allowed," Oskar said.

"Not really," Tilly said mutinously.

"Of course, we could do some quick detecting now, if you wanted," Gretchen said casually.

"What do you mean?" Tilly said, although she had a feeling she knew exactly what Gretchen meant.

"Well, I admire your bravery in wanting to go and find evidence of what that Chalk man is doing, and I think that, whatever age you are, you should be allowed to pursue what is right, and try to find the truth."

"Do you really think things are getting much worse very quickly?" Tilly asked.

"I'm only going on what I've seen so far," Gretchen said. "And I am worried about what is happening to our fairy tales. Will you help me protect them, Tilly?"

"Tilly and I are fine, thanks," Oskar said, climbing a few steps toward bed. Tilly stayed still.

"So, what, you think we could just pop in quickly, and see if we could find Chalk, or more about what Melville is doing?" Tilly said, moving toward Gretchen.

"Bad idea," Oskar said. "Definitely a bad idea."

"Yes, exactly," Gretchen said, ignoring Oskar. "We're not hunting anyone down. We'll maybe chat to some of the characters who've seen Chalk wandering around, and just observe—see if we spot anyone collecting book magic, or causing problems, and if we don't find anything, then nothing is lost, and we'll see what plan the others can come up with. What do you think?"

"And you promise we'll be able to come straight back? That we won't get lost in a different book?"

"We'll be incredibly careful," Gretchen said. "I promise."

"Honestly, this is a bad idea," Oskar repeated.

"Clara always says how brave her grandson is," Gretchen said. "But I understand if you'd rather get to bed."

"I'm only going if you come with me," Tilly said, looking at Oskar.

"I'm obviously not going to let you go by yourself," Oskar said, resigned. "Just promise I get to say I told you so if I'm right."

"Deal," Tilly said, and turned back to Gretchen. "Okay. We can try. But we're both coming, and any sign of anything really weird, and we're heading straight back."

"Of course," Gretchen said. "It's a research mission, nothing more. Shall we?" And Tilly realized the blue book she was already holding was a book of fairy tales.

"But we're in our pajamas," Tilly said.

"Well, it was good enough for Arthur Dent," Gretchen said.

"Who?" Tilly said, confused.

"*The Hitchhiker's Guide to the Galaxy*?" Gretchen said. "By Douglas Adams? You should read it one day. It contains the meaning of life."

"In a novel?" Tilly said.

"Where else would you find it?" Gretchen said, smiling. She held out her hand.

Tilly looked at Oskar, who was now struggling to keep a look of excitement off his face, and they linked hands, and took a deep breath.

As the shadows folded down around them, they found themselves shivering in the night air, regretting that they hadn't changed out of their pajamas.

"Where are we exactly?" Tilly said, teeth chattering.

"We're on the edge of 'Hansel and Gretel,'" Gretchen said. "Somewhere in there is the gingerbread house."

"The one where the witch who eats children lives?" Oskar said. "I thought we weren't going anywhere dangerous."

"Don't worry, we're not going to talk to the witch," Gretchen said. "This is just where I came last time when I heard people mentioning Chalk, so I thought it was a sensible place to start. Let's get out of the forest. Look, you can see the field through the trees."

They headed along the path into a grid of fields, which looked very similar to those that Tilly and Oskar had visited from the fairy-tale book in Paris. Except that here there was a large stone castle on a hill, complete with a turret and a drawbridge over a moat.

"Let's try there," Gretchen said, and they started heading in that direction. "Remember, we're just on the lookout for someone who could help."

"Speaking of people who might help," Tilly said, "I was talking to my mum about the Archivists and I was thinking that maybe they're from books, like the characters we meet? What do you think?"

"An interesting idea," Gretchen said, as they walked through the damp grass.

"You seemed pretty convinced that the Archivists are out there somewhere," Tilly said. "Why are you so sure? No one else seems to be."

"All stories are rooted in something real, even the most fantastical and impossible ones," Gretchen said. "Just like these fairy stories all grew from real people or ideas or feelings. I think that Archivists are based in fact. I'm just not sure who or where they are. I agree that they've been mythologized, but I firmly believe that something bigger than us exists out there to protect bookwandering and its fundamental nature. It has to. Something rooted in the history of stories and libraries and bookshops, to help us if we need it. The magic in books that lets us be part of them, and them part of us. I have to believe that if the world were in danger of ignoring the power of stories, or that people started thinking in terms of the limits of their bodies and not the scope of their imaginations, there is something, or someone, or a group of someones, who would do something. And I believe the Archivists are those someones."

"But whoever they are, what use are they if no one knows where they are or how to talk to them?"

"I believe they'd know when they were needed," Gretchen said. "Your theory is interesting, though. One of the rumors I've heard is that the Archivists have hidden themselves in layers and layers of books. It shouldn't be possible to travel into books inside books, but they may have found a way. Nothing is truly impossible inside a book."

"But that means there are infinite potential places they could be?" Oskar said.

"Yes," Gretchen said. "Goodness knows where you'd even start, if you didn't have any clues. I imagine you would need some kind of map, but . . . Hang on." She paused. "Can you hear something?"

Tilly stopped walking and listened.

"What is that?" she said, as the rumbling noise grew louder. "It sounds like a Tube train arriving at a station. . . ."

Suddenly, huge chunks of the ground around them started falling away into more of the black nothingness that they had seen behind the doors of the Seven Dwarfs' and the Three Bears' houses.

"Run!" Gretchen shouted.

Gretchen grabbed Oskar's and Tilly's hands, pulling them away from the crumbling ground and toward the castle. After a few moments the rumbling stopped, and they were at a safe distance from the holes in the ground. The three of them looked back from where they stood, breathing heavily. The moonlight illuminated the land, but seemed to sink straight into the holes and be absorbed entirely.

"What was that?" Tilly said. "Are they more plot holes?"

"That was why we were right to come tonight," Gretchen said. "Fairy tales are collapsing around us. I think this is even more serious than the odd plot hole. I think those are the stories crumbling away."

"What?" Tilly said. "Can that happen while we're inside a story?"

"Yes," Gretchen said, looking out at the broken landscape. "The fabric of these stories is fraying. I think that the Endpapers are starting to encroach on the stories as they decay around us. The Endpapers are there to hold stories together, as I'm sure you know, but I think this might be a side effect of the stories breaking. The Endpapers don't know what to hold together and where. I am sure the person we're going to visit can help."

"The person who told you about Chalk?" Oskar asked.

"Yes," Gretchen said. "I spoke to her last time I was here, and she was the first person who told me she'd seen him. Although I didn't know who he was at the time, of course."

"Well, it's somewhere to start," Tilly said.

The castle at the top of the hill stood cold and quiet against the night sky.

"It doesn't look very friendly," Tilly said nervously.

Gretchen pointed. "Look, the drawbridge is down, so they obviously don't mind visitors."

The trio walked across the creaking wooden bridge, and into a small courtyard. In one wall was a great oak door, and Gretchen strode over to it and took hold of a huge iron ring hanging from it, swinging it heavily against the wood. The knocking rang out into the still night air, and after a few moments, it swung open to reveal warm yellow light in the corridor, and the smell of something hearty cooking somewhere. The lack of anyone who had obviously opened the door felt rather ominous, but the comforting light and smell reassured Tilly and Oskar, and they followed Gretchen inside. The door swung shut behind them.

"This way," Gretchen said cheerfully, leading them down a stone corridor lit with torches hung in iron sconces on the wall. At the end of the corridor was a series of stone steps leading downward into darkness.

"This very much has a horror-film vibe," Oskar said, peering into the inky light.

"Don't worry, guys," Gretchen said. "Surely it takes more than a little darkness to frighten you?"

"It's more the combined effect," Oskar said. "You know, spooky castle, holes in the ground, doors opening on their own . . ."

In the end, there was nothing to do but follow Gretchen down, and at the bottom there was another door, which she confidently pushed wide open. They found themselves in a large room with no windows, lit by more torches and lined with benches heaving with piles of paper covered in complicated notes, and bottles full of black liquid. Tilly couldn't get the word "dungeon" out of her mind.

"Gretchen, my dear, how good to see you."

They heard a voice like honey, and from out of the shadows walked a tall, elegant woman dressed in a sweeping purple velvet dress with tight, long sleeves that ended in points that hooked around her middle fingers. Her blonde hair was piled up elaborately, and a long black lace veil hung from the back of it. Her lips were painted blood-red. She embraced Gretchen warmly as if greeting an old friend, then took the book of fairy tales from under her arm and laid it on a bench behind her.

"You know each other?" Oskar said, standing closer to Tilly.

"Yes," Gretchen said. "This is the woman who helped me before."

"Please take no notice of the getup," the woman said. "It's all part of the role. We stepmothers get the raw deal every time, never mind if we've never even glanced in a magic mirror or plotted to kill our stepdaughters."

"What's all this stuff in the bottles?" Tilly said, gesturing around. "Is that book magic?"

"Well spotted," the woman said.

"But how do you know what that is?" Tilly said suspiciously. "You're a fairy-tale character, right . . . ?"

"Tilly!" Gretchen reprimanded her. "Lady Vesper is helping us! There's no need to be so antagonistic."

"I'm sorry," Tilly apologized out of instinct, her horror of

being told off in front of other people overriding her sense of something being not at all right.

"Please don't worry," Lady Vesper said. "And there's no need to be so stern, Gretchen. It's a fair question with an easy answer. I did not even know that this was book magic until very recently when Gretchen arrived looking for help. I had been experimenting with this substance for years, not having any idea what it was. Then I realized it was everywhere now that my world had started to fall apart."

"So, what, you're a mad-scientist, non-evil stepmother?" Oskar said, and Lady Vesper laughed.

"Something like that," she said. "Now, was there something you came to ask on your way through? I promise you, there's no need to be so skittish, Tilly. Look, the door behind you is wide open. You're free to go anytime you'd like."

"We wanted to know if you had seen that man again," Gretchen said. "We think he might have something to do with all of this chaos."

"All of what chaos?" a voice said from behind them—and down the stairs and into the light walked Enoch Chalk.

28

All Part of the Plan

All trace of pleasantness immediately fell from Vesper's face. "What are you doing here, Chalk, you idiot?" she said, voice dripping with poison, as Tilly stared in horror at the man who had trapped her mother for eleven years.

"Have I come at the wrong time, my lady?" he said obsequiously, backing away.

"It's too late now, you fool," Vesper said. "Come back and lock the door behind you. At least we can do away with pretenses now that you're here." Chalk did as he was told, and pocketed the large iron key. Tilly's mind was racing.

"Were you in on this?" she said to Gretchen, who was looking somewhere between exhilarated and queasy.

"Don't worry, Tilly," she said. "This is all part of the plan."

"What plan? Whose plan?" Oskar said.

"Calm down, child," Vesper said. "It's considerably less dramatic than it seems. Let's sit down and talk this through. Chalk, will you find some wine and some honey wafers, please? Through there." She pointed at a door in the corner. "Come, let's all sit."

"I would not drink anything she gives you," Oskar whispered to Tilly.

"No kidding," Tilly said, glad Oskar was there too, even if it was her fault they were both in this situation.

Chalk brought out a tray of wine and delicate wafer biscuits and offered them to Vesper and to Gretchen.

"And the children," Vesper said, and Chalk, looking as though it was physically paining him, offered the tray to Tilly and Oskar, too. Tilly almost ate something just to spite him, but elected to ignore him instead.

"Can you please tell us what's going on?" Tilly said, while eyeing up the blue book of fairy tales they needed to escape, which was lying on the desk behind them.

"My name is not really Vesper," the woman said. "It is Decima. Decima Underwood. You may have heard of me."

"As in . . . You're Melville's sister? The one who died?" Tilly said.

"Half a point, Tilly," she said. "I had been told you were cleverer than this. I am clearly not deceased. But yes, I am Melville's sister."

"Why didn't you come back with him? What are you doing here?" asked Tilly in horror, a chill creeping down her spine as the chances of this ending well diminished second by second.

Decima stood tall. "We have unfinished business here, and

one of us needed to stay and attend to it. My brother drew the short straw."

"Why is going back to the real world the short straw?" Oskar asked, confused. "Why would you want to stay here?"

"Because he will begin to age as soon as he leaves," Decima said, shuddering at the thought. "Which is what I am working on. And despite his distaste for the aging process, he cannot deny that I am much better at the science side of things than he is. His skills lie, as I'm happy to admit, on the charm-offensive side."

"But what are you working on, and what does he have to do with it?" Oskar said, jerking his head in Chalk's direction.

"One thing at a time. Don't worry so much about him—he's really considerably less important than everyone seems to think," Decima said. "Firstly, we are working on something that we believe you might be able to help us with. That is why we asked Gretchen to accompany you here, which she has so kindly and so efficiently done for us." Tilly looked in horror at Gretchen, who couldn't even meet her eyes.

"You tricked us?" Tilly said.

"Not really," Gretchen said, having the grace to sound a little embarrassed. "I just fudged some of the details so you would come."

"What do you want?" Tilly said. "I'm not doing anything that helps him." She stared coldly at Enoch Chalk, trying not to let her fear show on her face.

"Perfectly understandable," Decima said. "But, no, I hope it's something that you'll happily agree to. I am trying to find a way to heal fairy tales—that's what all this paraphernalia is for. I'm trying to work out what is going on, and how to stop it. So, you see, we are not on opposing sides."

"So why didn't you just ask?" Tilly said. "And why me?"

"Well, Matilda," Decima said. "Let us lay all our cards out on the table. We know who your father is. We know that you are half-fictional, and that makes you special."

"I wouldn't go as far as special," Chalk said dismissively. "It's merely a biological quirk. Don't go inflating her already oversized ego."

Tilly turned to Decima. "Before we go any further," she said, "I want to know why he is here, because I won't help with anything that he will benefit from. He kept my mum trapped for eleven years."

Decima nodded. "Leave," she said to Chalk.

"What?" Chalk spluttered.

"I said, leave," she repeated. "Matilda's request is perfectly reasonable considering what you've put her family through and I think that if we are going to ask for her help she deserves a chance to properly weigh the situation up without your menacing presence hovering over her."

Chalk made a big show of walking very slowly to the door and slamming it behind him.

"I'm sorry, Tilly," Decima said. "He was a necessity. We wanted to know if we could use his information to help our quest."

"But you've been here for years, and he's only been here for a few months."

"Yes, but he makes himself useful, and we've gleaned some tidbits from him. Don't worry, he's a spare part in the greater battle."

Tilly did not trust her at all, but couldn't deny that she enjoyed seeing Chalk being put in his place. "So, what do you need me for?"

"Well, we have reason to believe that the fact that you are of both worlds—reality and fiction—means you might be the key."

"The key to what?"

"To healing fairy tales, of course," Decima said.

"Me?" Tilly said.

"Yes, you. You're unique, and therefore very important. And so I have a great favor to ask of you."

"Which is?" Tilly said hesitantly.

"A drop of your blood," Decima said.

"Okay, that is very much a red flag," Oskar said. "I'm not sure anything good ever came from giving blood in dungeons."

"Just a drop," Decima said, staring daggers at Oskar. "Nothing sinister. Just one tiny drop that we can mix with this book magic and use to reverse what is happening here in the fairy-tale lands."

"This is why you brought me here?" Tilly said to Gretchen.

"Yes," she said. "I'm so sorry for the subterfuge, I truly am, but I was worried that you would say no, or that you would tell your grandparents, and their love for you would blind them to the bigger story."

"And you trust her?" Tilly said. "Even though she's using Chalk?"

"Yes, I do," Gretchen said. "Although I didn't know about Chalk. But, Tilly, imagine if you could say you were the one to heal fairy tales. What a thing that would be. Think how proud your mum would be of you."

"Just one drop?" Tilly said.

"Yes." Decima nodded. "And your grandfather was a Librarian, wasn't he? So it is no more than he has done in the service of stories. You're carrying on the family legacy in a way."

"Tilly, I really think you should stop and think about it for a minute," Oskar said. "Can we just have a quick chat?"

"I'm afraid there isn't time for that," Decima said. "And it is Tilly's decision. Not mine or Gretchen's or yours."

"It can't do any harm, can it?" Tilly said to Oskar.

"Of course it can!" he said. "You saw the Librarians use Melville's blood to bind him to stories!"

"That's purely symbolic," Decima said. "It's just ink and blood; there's no book magic there."

"And we can go home after this, yes?" Tilly said.

"Of course," Decima said. "Gretchen can take you and . . . What's your name?"

"Oskar," he said. "Don't mind me."

"Great," Decima said. "You can just go and stand over there."

"I was being sarcastic," Oskar said under his breath, and stayed put by Tilly's side.

"So, what do you think, Tilly?" Decima said, taking a step closer.

Tilly took a deep breath.

"Okay," she said. "Let's give it a go."

Oskar opened his mouth as if to try to stop her but ended up just shrugging.

"It's your call, Tilly," he said in the end. Tilly steeled herself.

"If it will help stories, then I'll do it," she said.

And she held out her hand.

29

Evidence

Decima went over to a workbench and picked up a glass bottle of inky book magic, and a sharp silver pin with an ornate rose-shaped head.

"Just a little scratch," Decima said, gently holding Tilly's hand over the bottle and pricking her finger lightly with the pin. It felt like a tiny scratch and then it was done, and they all watched as two drops of blood fell into the magic below.

"Is it going to do something?" Oskar said.

"It's not some cheap trick," Decima said, voice annoyed but eyes focused on the vial.

"So can we go now?" Tilly said, holding her finger. "That's all you needed?"

"Well, potentially," Decima said. "But we need to make sure it's worked, of course. My brother should be here any second."

"What? How?" Tilly felt the horrid, creeping chill of fear again.

"Melville is keeping track," Decima said. "You're ever so lucky, Matilda, as you find yourself in a Source Edition. And as you know, anything we do here will be mirrored in all copies of the book. And this book has a very limited run; only two others exist. We gave one to Gretchen here so she could find us easily, and one has been at the Underlibrary with my brother so he can see what is happening here and knows the moment to . . ."

All of a sudden, Melville Underwood was standing in the middle of the room. But he didn't look anything like the last time Tilly had seen him. He was no longer the handsome, groomed man, but looked as though he had aged twenty years in only a few days.

"Oh, brother, reality not treating you well?" Decima smirked. "I might have been born first, but you are definitely the older twin now, I'd say."

Melville didn't laugh. "Is it done?" he said, not even acknowledging Tilly's presence.

"Let's find out, shall we?" Decima said. Melville stepped forward and took his shirt off, revealing that his entire body, except for his forearms, was covered in crude, faded tattoos. There didn't seem to be any discernible pattern to them; they didn't look much like the beautiful tattoos Tilly sometimes saw on customers in the bookshop. They were mainly lines and circles, and even what looked like messy writing, although Tilly couldn't see what it said from where she was.

Tilly and Oskar watched in increasing alarm as Decima produced a needle that was tied to a small wooden stick, and dipped it into the bottle of magic that had the drops of Tilly's blood in it. She then proceeded to make a series of tiny pokes in Melville's shoulder where there was still some untattooed skin, while Melville gritted his teeth.

"This doesn't look good," Oskar said.

"What are they doing?" Tilly whispered to Gretchen, who looked slightly nauseous watching them.

"I'm not sure, Tilly," she said. "She told me that this was all to save fairy tales."

"Well, why don't you go and ask them?" Oskar said. "As you seemed so confident of the plan. Or we can just leave? I don't want one of those tattoo things, thank you very much."

"No one is tattooing you," Gretchen said. "Either of you. Maybe you're right, and it is time to go." She went over to the door, but it was still locked from when Chalk had arrived.

"I'm afraid we need you to stick around for just a little while longer," Decima said, without taking her eyes from her brother's arm.

"Come, now, Decima," Gretchen said. "I've brought Tilly along as you asked, and she's been very willing to help—even if it isn't immediately obvious how whatever you are doing now is going to help fairy tales. So we'll just head back, and we can check in again later?"

"I'm afraid not," Decima said. "Now, don't annoy me while I have a needle in my hand." She went back to the tattoo, and Tilly nudged Oskar gently.

"We should try to take something back for Grandma and Grandad," she whispered very quietly. "They need evidence to convince all the other librarians. What can you grab?"

Oskar scanned their immediate vicinity and nodded subtly to Tilly's left, where there was a small pile of stoppered bottles full of book magic. Tilly nodded and stretched her hand out and picked up two delicate glass containers. She slid one into her pocket and gave the other to Oskar. It was only seconds later that Decima finished Melville's tattoo and wiped it roughly with a cloth.

"Anything?" Melville said impatiently. She peered at him.

"I can't see any changes," she said. "Look in the mirror."

"You *do* have a magic mirror," Oskar said.

"It's just a regular mirror, you imbecile," Decima said.

"No, no change," Melville said, staring at his face in the mirror. "You've done it wrong."

"I assure you I haven't," Decima said icily. "My research is accurate. The principles make sense. We just need to fine-tune."

"Well, get on with it, woman," Melville said. "Look at the state of me."

"Could you tell us how this is helping fairy tales?" Tilly tried again, although her hope that they had been telling the truth had all but evaporated.

"Silly girl," Decima said. "I couldn't care less about fairy tales. Your naivety is astonishing. I can't believe how easy it was to convince you that was the case. No wonder Gretchen got you here so easily. Do you believe everything you're told?" Tilly looked at Gretchen, who was looking very pale and now openly panicking.

"I had no idea," Gretchen said. "I'm so sorry, Tilly. I promise I'll get us out of here."

"Don't make promises you can't keep," Melville said. But he was interrupted by the same rumbling noise they had heard outside, and a huge crack splintered the floor underneath them, separating all of them from the door to the stairs. They watched in horror as the workbench holding the blue book they'd traveled in with toppled into it; but instead of falling and crashing, as soon as it touched the crack it just disappeared, as if being swallowed by a pool of oil. It was just like what had happened to the stone Jack had thrown into the dwarfs' cottage.

"Dammit," Melville said. "We need to hurry up and get out of here."

"Do you think I don't know that?" Decima snapped.

"So, just to be clear," Oskar said. "You are not interested in fixing . . . this?"

"No, boy," Decima said. "We're the ones who caused it."

This was the final straw for Gretchen, who got to her feet and stalked toward the twins.

"After all of this, you were the ones damaging fairy tales?"

"Yes," Decima said. "Of course. You of all people know how fragile fairy tales are. On one of our tours back in the day, we discovered, in a genuine accident, that if one . . . destabilizes them more on purpose, they start to simply leak book magic. Which of course is the most valuable resource there is and can be put to all sorts of uses."

"You're breaking fairy tales on purpose?" Tilly said, horrified.

"Yes," Melville said slowly, as if explaining something to a very small child. "If one consciously pushes between different collections, weaves in and out of the different layers, it weakens them, and makes it even easier for characters to move between stories. And that releases all this lovely book magic for us. I'll admit I didn't quite realize that the Endpapers would do . . . whatever they are doing," he said, gesturing at the gap in the floor. "So we need to work this out. Quickly," he said pointedly to Decima, as the room shook around them and the cracks in the floor widened.

"Okay," she said, focusing. "Well, I only used a few drops

before, so perhaps it is just a quantity issue and we need more."

"More?" Tilly said, scared. "More what?"

"More of you, clearly," Decima said. "Come here."

"Absolutely not," Oskar said.

"No," Tilly said. "And I still don't understand . . . What are the tattoos for?"

"One of the particularly lovely ways one can use book magic is to borrow some of its properties," Decima said, raising her voice over the ongoing rumbling as she sorted through piles of her research. "If one can get it into one's body, then one can absorb some of the immortal nature of our stories."

"Can't you just drink it?" Oskar said, horrified.

"We tried that, of course," Melville said, steadying himself against a wobbling table. "But it had only a transient effect. Tattoos are the most efficient method we've found so far. However, it would seem that they only work while we are inside stories. We have managed to stop ourselves aging here, but as you'll see from my face, it immediately stops working in the real world, and in fact my body seems to be trying to catch up with my biological age at double time. This is why we need Matilda."

"You are of stories and of the real world," Decima said. "And so infusing your essence with book magic should make our tattoos last long enough to at least slow this down so we can work out how to stop it forever."

"But why?" Tilly asked.

"I would have thought the appeal of immortality was

obvious," Decima said. "But I'm afraid the particulars of what we would like to achieve are not for your ears. I'm all for sharing the science you are participating in, Matilda, it seems only fair, but let's not get carried away. Now, are you going to help us willingly or not? Because we are very rapidly running out of time." At that, another crack splintered across the floor, and a sheaf of papers fluttered down into it, disappearing immediately.

"Obviously not," Tilly said, although she was not sure exactly what she could do to stop it.

"A shame," Decima said. "Although not entirely unexpected at this stage. But never mind, we really don't care either way." And she picked up a silver knife from the bench behind her.

"No," Gretchen said, and stepped forward, placing herself between Tilly and Oskar, and the twins. "This has gone far enough. What you are doing is reprehensible." And Tilly realized Gretchen was crying. "I will not let you harm Tilly in pursuit of whatever evil plan you have."

"Finally, a backbone," Decima sneered. "You were happy for us to use this child's blood for something that suited your goals, but not now?"

"Before I thought that it was to help heal fairy tales, not harm them!" Gretchen said. "And you just wanted one drop!"

"I'm not sure that's much better," Oskar said angrily, finding that he did not have much faith in Gretchen's ability to protect them.

"Who is the other one, again?" Melville said, noticing Oskar.

"Come on!" Oskar said. "I've been here the whole time!"

"He's my best friend," Tilly said. "And you can't touch him."

"How sweet. But I assure you we have no interest in him at all," Melville said.

"Rude," Oskar said, and Tilly looked at him in amazement.

"Are you saying you would rather be the person that two evil twins are trying to steal blood from?" she said.

"No, I'm just saying that it's a bit rude to say they don't care what happens to me," Oskar said. "But I agree perhaps it's not the most pressing issue, right at this moment." He turned back to the three adults, who were just staring at him. "Continue," he said.

"Anyway," Tilly said to the Underwoods. "People will notice that we're gone. You can't just kill me or keep me here or whatever you're planning."

"I'm sure that people will be ever so sad to hear that the two of you bookwandered with Gretchen and were sadly captured and eaten by the witch in the gingerbread house," Melville said. "To think that Archie and Elsie Pages were so careless as to let their only granddaughter bookwander with known rebel Gretchen Stein—such a tragedy."

"Right, enough of this," Gretchen said, squaring her shoulders and facing the twins.

"I don't think so," Melville said, stepping forward. And with an abrupt push to her shoulder, he sent Gretchen stumbling backward.

"No!" shouted Tilly in shock, jerking forward. But she wasn't fast enough and Gretchen toppled straight into the crack in the middle of the floor, where the darkness of the Endpapers immediately swallowed her up.

"What have you done?" Oskar said in horror. "Did you kill her?"

"Don't be ridiculous," Decima said. "It's just the Endpapers."

"But where will she go, the Underlibrary?" Tilly said.

"No, I'm afraid not."

"So where is she?"

"Oh, floating in an endless void, I would have thought," Melville said. "Don't worry, someone will be able to fish her out at some point probably." Melville's words unstuck something in Tilly's brain, and she grabbed Oskar's hand and edged backward.

"Do you trust me?" she asked him quietly.

"Do you even have to ask?" Oskar said, squeezing her hand. She took a deep breath and pulled Oskar backward and the two fell down into the Endpapers, eyes closed, and Melville and Decima had no time to do anything but watch them disappear.

After a few seconds the familiar wood and paper smell of the British Underlibrary reassured Tilly they were where she had expected.

"Don't even think about saying I told you so," she said to

Oskar in the gloom of the empty office where they had landed.

"I would never," he said.

"But I'd have to take it if you did," she admitted. "I'm sorry I took us there."

"You don't need to say sorry," he said. "I understand why you wanted to go. And we're safe. Ish. And they can't hide anymore now that we've seen them like that. What do we do now?"

"I guess we find a phone? And tell Grandma and Grandad?" Tilly said. "It's Christmas Eve—there won't be anyone around here." She ran her hands over the wall until she found a light switch that illuminated an old rotary phone on a desk. She breathed a sigh of relief as she picked up the receiver and heard a tone, then quickly dialed the number for home. "They won't have even noticed we're gone, I bet." But someone picked up on the very first ring.

"Matilda?" an urgent voice said.

"Hi, yes, Grandad, it's me!" she said. "Can you—"

"Where are you? Are you safe? Where have you been? Are you with Gretchen and Oskar?"

"I'm with Oskar at the Underlibrary," Tilly said. "We didn't think you'd have noticed we'd gone yet!"

"Matilda," her grandad said, his voice cracking. "It's Boxing Day. You've been missing for nearly two days."

30

An Enemy of British Bookwandering

"We've been so scared," Grandad said. "I would never have forgiven myself if something had happened to you, Tilly."

"We're fine, I promise," she tried to reassure him.

"Is my mum okay?" Oskar asked, sounding panicked.

"We have her here," Grandad said. "She's okay, or she will be now that we know where you are. We'll explain everything once we've got you back safe. And it sounds like you'll have a lot to tell us as well. Now, can you get to the Map Room?"

Grandad told Tilly and Oskar to make their way to the Map Room, where he and Amelia would meet them, via the secret magical passageway that linked the Underlibrary and Pages & Co.

"Keep out of sight," he instructed. "Amelia says there may be a few people working today, including Seb. If you get into hot water, just ask for him and say as little as possible until we're there. Okay?"

Tilly and Oskar crept out into the corridor and tried to get their bearings and make their way to the Map Room.

"How were we gone for two days?" Oskar said, looking shell-shocked. "And what will they have told my mum?"

"Do you think she'd believe the truth?" Tilly asked.

"I've no idea, but they must have told her something, otherwise she'd have gone straight to the police."

"What happens if she did go to the police?" Tilly said, terrified.

"I guess we'll find out." Oskar swallowed nervously. "But right now, we need to get out of here. I have a horrible sense of direction. Do you know where we're going?"

"I think left?" Tilly said.

"I still can't believe we were gone for days," Oskar repeated, not being able to wrap his head round it. "It only felt like an hour, if that."

"I know time goes all wonky in books," Tilly said. "But I've never heard of it happening like this, where time goes faster in real life."

"Probably because those Underwoods have messed everything up," Oskar said. "Will someone really be able to find Gretchen? I know she got us into that mess, but I'm not sure she deserves to be floating in . . . What did they call it?"

"An endless void," Tilly supplied.

"Right," he said, swallowing.

"I'm sure Amelia will be able to help," Tilly said, and even though Gretchen's betrayal was still sharp in her chest, she had to agree with Oskar that she didn't think she should be lost in the Endpapers forever as punishment. She reminded herself that she'd been taken in by the same lies that Gretchen had, as they rounded a corner and came eye to eye with a librarian. It was Angelica, the same young woman who had stamped Grandma and Grandad after the Inking Ceremony.

"What are you doing here?" she said nervously.

"Uhhh . . ." Tilly struggled to think of a good reason why they were wandering the corridors of the Underlibrary on Boxing Day.

"We're looking for Seb," Oskar said, remembering Grandad's instructions.

"Oh," Angelica said, still confused. "Well, he's in the meeting with everyone else—it's where I'm headed back to. I'll take you."

"Ah, don't worry," Tilly said. "We don't want to interrupt a big meeting!"

"But that's where Seb is."

"We can wait!"

"Are you sure you're supposed to be here?" she said slowly. "I think you should come with me."

Short of turning and running away, they weren't sure what else to do. They followed Angelica down the corridor to a large room where fifteen or so librarians were sitting around a table, listening intently to Melville Underwood. He still looked middle-aged but calm and clean, with no sign that moments before he had been getting tattooed in a castle by his supposedly dead sister. He looked up as they came in, but barely reacted.

"Why are there children here, Angelica?" he asked. "And in their nightclothes, it would seem."

Tilly had entirely forgotten they were still wearing pajamas and slippers, and blushed as everyone stared at them.

"I just found them wandering around," Angelica said. "They said they were looking for Seb." All the heads at the table turned to stare at Seb, who was looking intently at Tilly, and she assumed that he knew that they had been missing for the last two days. He gave a tiny tilt of his head, as if to ask if they were okay, and Tilly gave a minute nod back.

"Sorry to interrupt," Tilly said. "We'll go now."

"Don't worry," Melville said smoothly. "No need to leave. Take a seat here and we can get you back home afterward."

Unsure of what else to do, they sat down.

"Now, as I was saying before we were interrupted," Melville continued. "I have wonderful news for you all. I am delighted and relieved beyond words to be able to share with you, my dear friends, that after many years, I have heard from my long-lost sister, Decima, whom we all believed to have been killed in the fairy-tale world."

Tilly and Oskar exchanged confused and worried looks.

"In what feels like a miracle, not only has she managed to hide herself away in a corner of a fairy tale and survive these long years, but also to discover a way to communicate with us in the stories. And through this we know that she has done what I could not, and managed to find and subdue Enoch Chalk. . . ."

"What?" Oskar hissed at Tilly, which earned him stares from Melville and Seb, for very different reasons.

"In fact," Melville went on, "I believe that she will be able to bring him to justice any . . . second . . . now." And as he said it, the door swung open to reveal Decima Underwood, not dressed in her rich purple velvet robes, but in a ripped and dirty plain brown dress, with her hair tied up in a rag. Behind her was Enoch Chalk, looking smug.

"Seize him!" Melville shouted, and there was instantly chaos, as the assembled librarians had no idea what to do, and Chalk himself looked around to try to work out who was being seized. Eventually two librarians half-heartedly held on to his sleeves, and Chalk spluttered in indignation.

"What is this charade, Melville?" he said.

"We hold you here under suspicion of threatening the very fabric of our stories, of killing a librarian in your escape from your Source, of holding a dearly loved bookwanderer hostage and away from her daughter, of attempting to steal a life for yourself, and of evading return to your Source Edition. You are also under suspicion of willfully damaging fairy tales for your own ends. How do you plead?"

"Well, guilty," Chalk said. "But you knew about all of that."

"Of course, we all knew of your crimes," Melville said. "And now you must answer for them."

"I am perplexed, friend," Chalk said, his face taking on a green hue as he realized that he had walked into a trap that he didn't quite understand. "We have been working together these past months, have we not?"

"Look at the lies he weaves to try to weasel his way out of the consequences of his actions," Melville said imperiously. Chalk started to wriggle in the hands of the librarians holding him, who held on more tightly.

"You promised that you would help me!" Chalk said. "You swore to me that you would share some of your book magic so I could finally be free of the magic that binds me to one book. I was promised her blood!" he said, glaring at Tilly.

A gasp went around the room.

"And so you incriminate yourself further," Melville said, pityingly. "And reveal that not only were you trying to misuse book magic for your own aims, but worse, you had plans to use the blood of a child as well?"

"What is this façade, Melville?" Chalk spluttered. "What do you gain by using me so ill?"

"There is no personal gain here," Melville said. "Only me, fulfilling the promises I made on my election day to bring you to justice for the crimes you have just confessed to in front of all of these witnesses."

"You," Chalk said, jerking a hand at Tilly and Oskar. "You can tell them I'm not lying." It was as if the words were knives in his throat, having to ask Tilly for help, but he was desperate. "Go on, child," he urged. "You were just there; you saw what they did and what they said."

Tilly and Oskar stayed silent, for they had no idea what to do. They knew Melville was lying, but to side with Chalk was unfathomable. The rage that had burned inside Tilly since she found out what Chalk had done to her mother was burning brightly, and she would not say a single word that would help him.

"I don't understand," Chalk said, realizing Tilly would not help, and trying to sound calm and friendly again. "Melville, my friend, can we speak outside, perhaps?"

"I am not your friend," Melville said coldly. "You are an enemy of British bookwandering. Your lies will not hold here anymore."

"How dare you speak to me like this!" Chalk said, flipping back to anger. "It is time to end this charade." He turned to the other librarians, who were in a state of confusion. "My friends," he tried. "I know that I kept things from you while I was your colleague, but many of us worked alongside each other for years and years, and I have only ever had the best interests of protecting books at heart, I swear to you. All I wanted was what you all have—a life. This man, who stands before you, lying so easily, he and his sister have been hiding me for the last few months. It is they who are stealing book magic!"

The atmosphere in the room was deeply unsettled, but Chalk's crimes were many and known, and the betrayal the assembled librarians felt was palpable. So no one spoke in his defense.

"You are simply parroting back my accusations!" Melville said. "And we are out of time. My friends," he turned to the other librarians, "you are satisfied that this man is Enoch Chalk, and that he has confessed to many and varied crimes against British bookwandering?" The librarians assented, for none of it was possible to deny. Melville nodded and reached into the inside pocket of his suit jacket and drew out a plain brown book.

"How did you get that?" Chalk said, fear written across his face. "That's mine."

"It is not yours," Melville said. "It belongs to the Underlibrary and its gatekeepers. But regardless, the time has come for your story to end." And without another word, and with no warning or ceremony, Melville tossed the book into the fire burning behind him.

Chalk let out a scream like nails down a blackboard, and everyone in the room shuddered at the awful sound. The two men holding his arms backed away, and Chalk stared at his hands in disgust as they started to blacken and smoke. Black rivulets of liquid started pouring from his eyes and ears.

Tilly thought she might be sick, but she could not look away. The whole room watched in silent horror as Chalk's skin seemed to turn into parchment before their eyes, and crackled and burned at the same rate as the book in the fire. The smell in the room was not of burning flesh, but of burning paper, and it did not take long before Chalk was no longer a man, but a small heap of smoldering ashes on the floor.

31

The Crux of the Matter

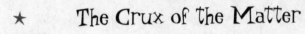

As the embers died away, two things happened: Decima Underwood fell into a dramatic faint, and the door burst open and in came Grandad, Amelia, and Bea.

"Melville Underwood, I knew we would catch you at it!" Amelia shouted. Seb shook his head desperately at her, aware that the mood of the librarians was firmly on Melville's side since he had brought Chalk to justice. Grandad rushed over to Tilly and Oskar, making sure they were okay.

"Ms. Whisper," Melville said. "You were not invited to this meeting. And, Mr. Pages, you are not welcome in the Underlibrary; I thought I made that very clear. And you"—he turned to Bea—"must be the daughter. It should go without saying, but you are not authorized to be here either. Can someone lock up our Sources, especially those with eligible men in them?" Melville said nastily. He clearly expected a response, but from the silence it became clear that Grandad's revoked access had not been made common knowledge.

"When our granddaughter has been missing for two days, I could not give two hoots about your daft new rules," Grandad said.

"You didn't know where your granddaughter was for two days—over Christmas?" Melville said, managing to make it sound like this was gross negligence on their part.

"No, it wasn't like that," Tilly said to the room. "We were bookwandering and time was lasting longer than it was supposed to! Because they"—she pointed at Melville, still kneeling beside Decima—"are breaking the fairy tales! What Chalk said was true!"

"Then why didn't you say anything earlier?" a librarian asked, genuinely confused, and Tilly looked up to see Cassius staring at her. "Why did you let Chalk be destroyed if he was telling the truth?"

"Because he did do all those awful things too!"

"So who are you claiming is lying, child?" Cassius said.

"Both of them were!" Tilly said. "But what Chalk was saying about Underwood is true! They're breaking stories on purpose so they can steal the book magic!"

"That is quite a claim to make against the Head Librarian, little girl," Cassius said patronizingly. "And I see you're tagging along. Again," he said, looking at Oskar, who glared right back.

"We have proof!" Oskar shouted, and went to grab the vial of book magic, patting his pockets down but finding nothing there. "I swear I had it in the story!" he said, to smirks from the librarians.

"What a foolish child," Melville said. "He expects to be able to bring things out of their stories. It's a good job that what-ever you tried to steal must stay in its place," he said. "Good for you, I mean." And even though Tilly could feel the hard glass of the bottle in her pocket, she kept silent, praying Oskar would understand why.

"Is that all?" Melville said. "We've heard a lot of nonsense, but there's no evidence—of anything! As far as I can see, we have a hanger-on from goodness knows where, a disgraced former Librarian—sorry, two disgraced former Librarians—and the meddling child of a bookwanderer and a *fictional character* sug-gesting . . . what exactly?"

The room froze at the mention of Tilly's parents.

"What did you say, Melville?" Cassius said.

"Oh, had they been keeping that from you as well?" Melville said silkily. "Why yes, Matilda's father is Captain Crewe from the beloved children's classic *A Little Princess*. You are all aware, I am sure, of Beatrice Pages's exploits twelve years ago, but it would appear that she was more successful than many of you know. After her failed attempt to permanently alter a Source Edition for her own selfish gains, she found a way to return to the man and, well, nine months later, there was a new bookwanderer. Archie and Elsie have obviously kept this information from you."

"It's family business," Grandad said. "Nothing to do with any of you."

"The child of a Librarian having a half-fictional child is nothing to do with the Underlibrary?" Melville said mockingly.

"Yes," said Bea with a steady voice, speaking for the first time. "What I do with my life is nothing to do with you. And if you choose to listen to the ramblings of this power-crazed man over my dad, well, then you have what you deserve."

"Then it seems that we are all content," Melville said. "You know the way out?"

"I'm going to find the Archivists and tell them what you're doing!" Tilly shouted over her shoulder, and to her horror the whole room burst into laughter.

"Why don't you tell the Tooth Fairy at the same time?" Melville smirked. "It'll be about as much use."

"But . . . !" Tilly said, face burning with embarrassment.

"Wait until we're home," Grandad said. He turned to Melville as they left. "You won't get away with this," he promised.

"And yet, you said that the last time I saw you, Archibald, and it remains unclear exactly what you think I'm getting away with."

"Shame on you all," Amelia said to the assembled librarians. "Think about which side of bookwandering history you want to be on." But she was met with silent, stony faces.

As they had been escorted out of the Underlibrary by Angelica, it was felt best that they didn't try to travel via the Map Room, and it was a subdued journey home in a taxi as Tilly and Oskar relayed everything they had seen.

"So, what I don't understand is how they were all communicating?" Tilly asked.

"Decima said you were in a Source Edition?" Amelia replied, and Tilly nodded. "Well, what I imagine they've done is create their own new book: a collection of other people's fairy tales most likely, but a new version so they have the Source. And of course, anything that happens in a Source is mirrored in every other version, so anyone else with a copy would be able to see immediately what was happening and read themselves in."

"I knew that book was familiar," Oskar said. "The blue one that Gretchen had? It's the same book that Chalk disappeared into."

"Oh, of course," Amelia said. "I can't believe I didn't work all this out sooner. Chalk and the Underwoods have clearly been speaking through those books for much longer than we imagined. Goodness knows how long he was under their thumb and helping sow seeds of discontent at the Underlibrary, rallying the Bookbinders against me. And then he went rogue, became fixated on Bea, and you, Archie, and so they just got rid of him. And poor Gretchen."

"But we'll be able to get her back, won't we? She did try to stop Decima when she realized what was really going on."

"Yes," Amelia said. "We'll get Seb on the case. Don't worry, we'll find her. And then we can deal with her."

"Will she be okay?"

"Well, we're not very sure," Amelia said honestly. "But we'll get Seb down to the Endpaper Processing Office first thing tomorrow and start there."

"Never mind all that," Oskar said. "What on earth did you tell my mum?"

"Ah," Amelia said. "All things considered she took it quite well, I think."

They got back to Pages & Co. to find Mary sitting at the kitchen table, glassy-eyed and shell-shocked. She didn't even get up when Tilly and Oskar came in, just stared at them as though they were changelings.

"Mary's obviously still processing the news," Grandma said gently, replacing the cold cup of tea in front of Mary with another hot and heavily sugared one. Oskar went over to her, close to tears, and tried to hug her.

"I'm sorry I didn't tell you, Mum," he said. "But you wouldn't have believed me! Archie and Elsie have been looking after me the whole time, I promise!"

"I . . . I . . ." Mary didn't manage to get any words out.

"It's because of Mamie!" he went on.

"Your grandmother knew the woman who took you into that place?" Mary said, finally speaking.

"But she didn't know what she was really like!" Oskar protested.

"How did you get Mary to believe?" Tilly said quietly to Grandad as Oskar tried to reassure his mother.

"Well, when you two disappeared, she obviously wanted to go straight to the police, and the only thing we could think of to stop her was to tell her the truth. And we thought the only way to do that was, well, show her."

"You took her bookwandering?" Tilly said.

"Yes! We had to under the circumstances! We just popped into somewhere nice and relaxing. We took her into *The Wind in the Willows*; we had a lovely picnic on the riverbank with Ratty and Mole, although she wasn't very relaxed, and we didn't stay long, but eventually she accepted it was really happening. I think making polite conversation with a mole while eating sandwiches helped convince her. And obviously, even though she didn't want to go to the police anymore, she was hardly more calm about you two being missing. Telling

her an errant bookwanderer had taken you goodness knows where is not exactly better news, but thankfully she trusted us to find you, and thank goodness we did. I've never wished you'd been stamped more."

They looked over at Mary, who was now holding Oskar tightly, still looking absolutely bemused. Eventually Amelia took the two of them off to try to answer Mary's questions, which, now that she was speaking again, were coming thick and fast.

"So what do we do now?" Tilly asked as she sat at the table with her grandparents and her mother.

"Well," Grandma said. "We need more information about what they are trying to do."

"Besides be immortal and in charge of everything forever?" Tilly said.

"I'm guessing that there are some specifics to the plan," Grandma said. "Although, yes, that does seem to be the crux of it."

"We need to have enough proof that we can convince the Underlibrary not to trust the Underwoods," Grandad said. "They've been very clever at manipulating everyone, and using your identity as a weapon, Tilly. We need to tread carefully and work out how to turn the tide. And hope we can think of something before they start binding books."

"For now," Grandma said, "the most important thing is to look after each other. Shall I put the kettle on?"

Tilly nodded. But she couldn't quite silence the niggling voice in her head saying that they were missing something important. In her bedroom, lined up on the top of her bookshelf, were a key, a vial of book magic, a bag of bread crumbs, a book, a ball of red thread, and a slip of paper that mentioned the Library of Congress in America. Some of which she'd found, and some of which had been given to her. She couldn't help but think that if she somehow put them together, they might show her a different way to look at bookwandering.

Epilogue

Three Months Later

Life had settled back into its normal rhythms as they monitored what was going on at the Underlibrary. They heard, via Seb, that there was still talk of everything Melville had threatened, and yet nothing seemed to have been put into place. Tilly knew that the adults hoped that maybe it wasn't as extreme as they'd first worried it was, and maybe they could just ride out Melville's tenure as Head Librarian without too much drama. Even Tilly's enthusiasm for finding clues in the pamphlet had waned, as it really was just a history of libraries in very small writing. And so life went on, and before she knew it, it was the Easter holidays, and she and Grandad were sitting reading next to each other in Pages & Co., enjoying the last of the evening sun as birdsong drifted in through the open bookshop windows.

"Is your book any good?" Grandad asked her as he paused to take a sip of coffee.

Tilly showed him the cover. She'd been using the scrap of

paper with the zip code and mysterious other number on it to keep her place in the book that Colette had given her to remind her of Paris, and it fluttered to the floor as she held the book up.

"What's that, then?" Grandad said, picking up the slip. "Why are you using a classmark as a bookmark?"

"A classmark?" Tilly repeated.

"That's what this looks like," Grandad said, pointing to the long string of numbers and letters. "It's how you find books in a library. This sequence will take you to a specific section or shelf or even book, depending on the subject. They're like maps, I suppose, to help you find what you need. Where did you get this one?"

"I found it in a book," Tilly said.

"I wonder where it leads," Grandad said, smiling. "We'll have to look it up. A little literary treasure hunt." He called up a website that listed all the classmarks and searched for the right number. "Here we go," he said. "It takes us to . . . Oh, interesting, ancient literary history! Was it a library book you found this in?"

"No . . ." Tilly said slowly. "What did you say about maps?"

"That classmarks are like maps?" Grandad repeated. "They take you where you need to go to find what you're looking for."

Tilly had that horrible feeling where a thought flashes through your head too fast for you to grab hold of it, and it's lost immediately, leaving only a shadow. As she was trying to claw it back, the peace was shattered abruptly as Seb burst into Pages & Co. in a panic, shouting for Grandma and Grandad.

"They've done it," he said.

"What do you mean?" Grandad said, standing up.

"They've finally done it," Seb said, out of breath. "They've convinced the librarians—they're going to start binding books tomorrow."

"Well, we knew it was coming," Grandma said, walking out of the kitchen, Amelia right behind her. "Even if we had hoped it would not."

"But we haven't any hard evidence yet," Seb said, flustered. "And we can't bookwander without being followed or watched! What are we going to do?"

Tilly was still staring at the piece of paper in her hand as they tried to calm Seb down. On one side was the address that she and her mum had worked out led to the Library of Congress in Washington, DC, and on the other was the classmark leading them to a specific book. Tilly had the feeling you get when you go into a room looking for something, but forget what it is when you arrive. And then it was there.

She went to find Bea.

"Mum?" she said.

"Yes?" Bea said. "Everything okay?"

"I think I know where to find the Archivists."

Once Upon a Time...

In Paris, Tilly and Oskar explore the unpredictable world of fairy tales, a place where the usual bookwandering rules don't quite apply. For bookwanderers, this is because fairy tales, like myths or folk stories, aren't rooted in one Source Edition. And, if you read fairy tales, you'll discover lots of different versions of the same stories and characters—you never know if you're going to find a happy ending or not. . . .

Most of the fairy tales that are familiar to us today have grown out of hundreds of years of storytelling from all over the world. Some researchers think they were even being shared in the Bronze Age—that's over 5,000 years ago! There are references to fairy tales being told among all different kinds of people for thousands of years.

A lot of the famous fairy tales we know today were collected by storytellers who went in search of their favorites. Some of the best-known fairy-tale collectors are the Brothers Grimm,

two German real-life brothers called Jacob and Wilhelm, who published a collection of stories called *Children's and Household Tales* in two parts, first in 1812 and then in 1815. Stories such as "Rapunzel" and "Hansel and Gretel"—two stories Tilly and Oskar encounter—were printed in these books for the first time.

Another celebrated collector was a Danish writer, Hans Christian Andersen, who wrote down a whopping 3,381 fairy tales over his life, some of which he wrote entirely himself, including popular stories like "The Emperor's New Clothes" and "The Ugly Duckling."

When Tilly and Oskar first bookwander into a fairy tale together, they visit a version of "Little Red Riding Hood"—a story with a lot of different versions, characters, and endings. There are records of it being told as long ago as the tenth century in France, and it possibly has roots in East Asian stories about a tiger grandmother.

Tilly and Oskar visit the first known printed version, which was created by a French writer called Charles Perrault in 1697. However, this one usually has a rather gory ending—which, luckily for Tilly and Oskar, an errant version of Red Riding Hood stops from happening. Many important collections of fairy tales originated in France. Gretchen's shop, the Faery Cabinet, is actually named after a famous illustrated French book of stories called *Le Cabinet des fées* from the eighteenth century. It was published in a huge forty-one volumes by a man called Charles-Joseph de Mayer.

In recent decades, filmmakers such as Disney have used fairy tales as a basis for some of their films, and have created their own versions. *Frozen* is inspired by Hans Christian Andersen's "The Snow Queen," and *Tangled* is of course a retelling of "Rapunzel."

Fairy tales are constantly evolving and changing as readers want different things from stories; and that's what makes them dangerous for a bookwanderer, but fascinating for readers and writers. Maybe you could even write one of your own. . . .

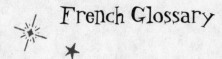

French Glossary

On y va!	Let's go!
Mon cher	My dear
Bonne nuit	Good night
On est gâté!	We're spoiled!
Et qui est-ce?	And who is this?
Oui	Yes
Non	No
Merci	Thank you
Mamie	Granny
Qui êtes-vous?	Who are you?
Dîtes-moi!	Tell me!
Maintenant!	Now!
Je suis anglais	I am English
Mais oui	But yes/but of course
Mes amis	My friends

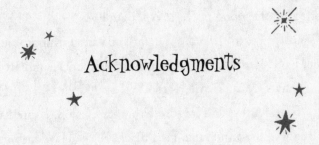

Acknowledgments

Thank you to my family: to my mum and dad, whom this book is dedicated to, for their love and support. To my sister, Hester; my grandparents; and the extended Kitchens and Brays. And to the Cottons/Colliers/Bishops/Rices.

Thank you to Adam Collier, who has been a constant source of encouragement, support, proofreads, and love.

Thank you to Claire Wilson, the wisest and most wonderful of agents. Thank you, always, to Sarah Hughes.

Thank you to everyone at HarperCollins Children's Books. In particular, thank you to my editor, Rachel Denwood—I don't know what I'm going to do without you. Your care, insight, and sense of humor have been a dream, and I've learned so much from you. Thank you also to Yasmin Morrissey, Nick Lake, Anna Bowles, Samantha Stewart, Julia Sanderson, Louisa Sheridan, Jo-Anna Parkinson, Jess Dean, Sam White, Elisa Offord, Beth Maher, Alex Cowan, David McDougall, Elorine Grant, Francesca Lecchini-Lee, Carla Alonzi, and Ann-Janine Murtagh.

Thank you to Paola Escobar for her beautiful illustrations and bringing the world of Pages & Co. to life.

Thank you to my friends for many and various things: Laura Iredale, Ruth Heatley, Jo Kitchen, Naomi Kent, Naomi Reed, Sarah Richards, Cat Doyle, Katie Webber, Kevin Tsang, Eve Tsang, Kiran Millwood Hargrave, Tom de Freston, Laure Eve, Kate Rundell, Rosalind Jana, Paul Black, Reece Haydon Black, Chris Smith, Anne Miller, Lizzie Morris, Jamie Wright, Jon Usher, Jen Herlihy, Lucie Mussett, Sarah Worth, Amy Stutz, Erin Minogue, Eric Anderson, Sarah McKenna, Matt Fairhall, and Lex Brookman.

Thank you so much to the bookshops, librarians, teachers, and bloggers who have read and written about and supported the books.

And most of all thank you to the readers of Pages & Co. It means everything to me that this story has meant something to you.

TURN THE PAGE FOR A LOOK AT

Tilly AND Oskar's

NEXT BOOKWANDERING ADVENTURE . . .

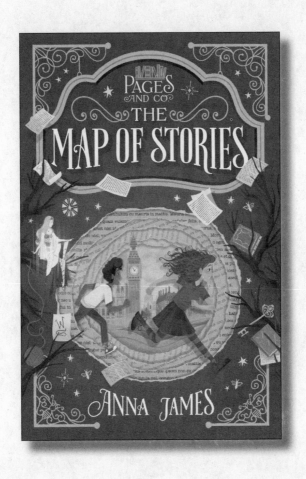

1

A Proper Plan

"I'm looking for a book."

Matilda Pages and her grandad looked up from writing recommendations cards for the shelves to see a man standing in front of them at the counter of Pages & Co. The shop was quiet as golden-hour sunlight dripped in through the tall windows so everything felt sleepy and peaceful.

"Well, we can definitely help you with that," Grandad said, glad of a customer. "Which book was it?"

"I can't quite remember the title, I'm afraid," the man went on. "Or the author, now I come to think about it. But I know that it has a blue cover. Or at least I think so."

"Can you remember *anything* about what's inside?" Grandad said encouragingly. Tilly grinned: she loved watching him work out which book someone wanted from whatever tiny bits of information they could remember.

"Not really . . ." the man said vaguely. "How strange! I

came to the shop specifically to pick this book up—it was my favorite when I was little, or was it my mum's favorite? It slips my mind. And now I'm here I can't remember the first thing about it. Maybe it wasn't so special after all . . ."

"Sounds like it meant a lot to you once upon a time," Grandad said. "I'm sure I can make some educated guesses if you can remember anything at all, or maybe we could help you find something different to read?"

"That's very kind of you," the man said politely, although he was already glancing back at the door. "But honestly—and I know this is the wrong thing to say in a bookshop—I just don't seem to care anymore."

Grandad raised an eyebrow.

"I'm sorry, I don't mean to be rude," the man went on. "It's just the more I think about it, the more I'm confused about what I even came in for."

"A book," Grandad reminded him. "With a blue cover."

"I'm not sure it even was blue," the man said, shrugging. "Oh well, thank you for your help." And with that he was gone.

"How peculiar," Grandad said.

"People can't remember what they're looking for all the time though," Tilly pointed out.

"Yes, but usually if they've bothered to make it into the bookshop they're a little more persistent, sometimes even quite annoyed that we can't immediately identify what they're looking for. *He* just seemed to forget what he even wanted as we spoke."

"Actually, there was another customer like that," Tilly said, remembering. "The other day a woman was just standing staring at a bookshelf for about ten minutes, not picking up any books or anything, and when I asked if I could help her find something, she said she wasn't sure, and then wandered off."

"Yes, very strange," Grandad said, but his attention had been distracted by a list of numbers on the screen of the till, his brow furrowed in concern. "Well, let's hope it's not a trend," he said. "We've been selling fewer and fewer books over the last couple of months. Maybe it's just that it's finally getting warmer and people are getting excited about being outside. As if we didn't have enough to worry about. How are you coping without bookwandering?"

"I hate it," Tilly said vehemently. "I hate that I can't do it, and that I can't talk to Anne or bookwander with Oskar, and most of all I hate that the Underwoods could just take it away without asking."

Since Melville Underwood had become the Head Librarian at the British Underlibrary, and made his sister, Decima, his official advisor, they had made good on their threats to limit bookwandering. They had promised, in a series of very formal statements, that it was only a short-term measure to keep bookwandering safe while they got to grips with their new roles, but the Pages family had very little trust in statements or promises from the siblings.

"Remind me how bookbinding works?" Tilly said. "Why did somebody even invent that in the first place?!"

"It was the Bookbinders," Grandad explained. "The group of librarians years and years ago who first wanted to try to limit who could bookwander. They use book magic to do it: that black sticky stuff you saw when the Underwoods were breaking up the fairy tales. It's barbaric really, what uses they put book magic to—the very opposite of where it comes from."

"But how does it work? Have you ever done it?"

"Books should only be bound in the most serious of situations," Grandad said. "And some would say never at all. While I was in charge at the British Underlibrary, we only bound a book once, and I'm still not certain it was the right thing to do. The process itself is fairly simple, however. All you have to do is trace an X of book magic over the first word of a book's Source Edition and it's like locking the door."

"So the Underwoods have done that to all the Source Editions?"

"All the ones at the British Underlibrary, it would seem. Although knowing them, they've got some of their underlings to do it. No doubt some of the librarians who have gleefully revived the Bookbinders name. But don't worry, Tilly, we'll think of something soon."

"I don't understand why you're so calm about it," Tilly said, the anger at having her freedom to bookwander stripped from her still prickling under her skin.

"I'm not at all calm about it," Grandad replied. "I'm as angry as you are, but it's too big a fight to just wade into and cause more problems. We have to make sure the Sources are protected at all times, as well as the people working at the Underlibrary. We need a proper plan."

"I *suggested* a proper plan," Tilly said mutinously.

"I know you think that . . . I mean, I understand that you believe . . ." Grandad faltered under the apparent strain of trying to say what he meant . . . without actually saying what he meant.

"I know you don't believe me that the Archivists are real, or that I know how to find them," she said. "You don't need to explain again. You're not going to convince me, though. Two separate people told me and Oskar that they use maps to tell you where they are—and I'm sure I've been sent one."

"You weren't given a map, sweetheart," Grandad said gently. "You found a collection of items that you think are linked together, because you want to be able to help. And we love you so much for that, but it's too great a risk to follow those clues . . . well, we *couldn't* even follow them. Where would we even start?"

Tilly rolled her eyes. "We start at the Library of Congress, in America," she explained, as if speaking to a child who wasn't paying attention. "That's where the first clue said to go. It had a . . . what did Mum call it, an American postcode?"

"A zip code," Grandad said.

"Right, a zip code!" Tilly said. "And it had a library classmark—you said yourself that classmarks are like maps—that's how I knew!"

"We can't fly all the way to America to find a book, Tilly," Grandad said. "Now give me a few moments of quiet so I can look through these sales numbers again. Why don't you go and find your mum, there's a good girl."

One of the things that Tilly loved most about her grandparents was that they almost always spoke to her like she was a proper person who understood things, and felt things, and had good ideas. But it meant it stung even more when they spoke down to her, as though she was just too young to understand what they were dealing with.

She stood up without saying anything else, meaning to go and find Bea and talk to *her* about the map, but before she could wander over to the stairs, the phone behind the counter started ringing.

"Good morning, Pages & Co.," Grandad said. "Archie

speak—Oh, Seb, hello, any news? Oh . . . Right . . ." He looked up to check Tilly hadn't gone and held a hand out to tell her to stay put. "I've got her here," he said down the phone, and Tilly felt a wave of fear crash over her. Grandad slammed the phone down and dragged her toward the door that connected the bookshop to where the Pages family lived.

"What are you doing?" she asked, trying to wriggle out of his grasp. "You're hurting me, Grandad!"

"I'm sorry, Tilly," he said. "But we need to get you hidden. Right now. That was Seb. The Underwoods are on their way here—and it's you they want."

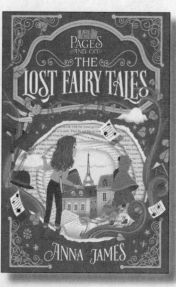